IRON HORSE PRIZE
KATIE CORTESE, SERIES EDITOR

Also in the series:

*The Birthright of Sons: Stories*
by Jefferey Spivey

*Lucky Bodies: Essays*
by Marianne Jay Erhardt

*Sing with Me at the Edge of Paradise: Stories*
by Joe Baumann

# Świnica

## and Other Stories

## Paul Linczak

TEXAS TECH UNIVERSITY PRESS

This book is typeset in Adobe Caslon Pro. The paper used in this book meets the minimum requirements of ANSI/NISO Z39.48-1992 (R1997). ⊗

These stories originally appeared, two in slightly different form, in the following publications: "Curtain Velvet" in *The Saint Ann's Review*; "The Death House" in *Evergreen Review*; and "Frankenstorm" in *The Carolina Quarterly*.

Designed by Hannah Gaskamp
Cover design by Hannah Gaskamp

Library of Congress Cataloging-in-Publication Data

Names: Linczak, Paul author. Title: Świnica: and Other Stories / Paul Linczak. Other titles: Świnica (Compilation) Description: Lubbock, Texas: Texas Tech University Press, 2026. | Series: Iron Horse Prize | Summary: "A collection of ten stories often dealing, among other human-interest topics, with the Eastern European immigrant experience"—Provided by publisher.
Identifiers: LCCN 2025040736 (print) | LCCN 2025040737 (ebook) | ISBN 978-1-68283-284-4 paperback | ISBN 978-1-68283-285-1 ebook
Subjects: LCGFT: Short stories Classification: LCC PS3612.I53247 S95 2026 (print) |
LCC PS3612.I53247 (ebook)
LC record available at https://lccn.loc.gov/2025040736
LC ebook record available at https://lccn.loc.gov/2025040737

Texas Tech University Press
Box 41037
Lubbock, Texas 79409-1037 USA
800.832.4042
ttup@ttu.edu
www.ttupress.org

# Contents

---

## I.

## II.

# Świnica

# I.

# Curtain Velvet

---

This was 2004. It was July Thursday, so of course was no
school. I was on job at this rich guy's house—I finish it his
basement for him. There I cut it my thumb with carpenter
knife. I forgot to put it first aid kit in my van, so I had to wrap thumb
with shirt and go home. I was bleeding lot, but it was be easy: just get
it the bandage and that's it. But when I come home I see it bicycle in
the yard. Then I knew I gonna meet one of Matthew's friends.

Matthew is my son. When I was young man I thought I gonna
have it four sons—Matthew, Mark, Luke, and John. But God gave
me him only.

I opened front door and saw him in my chair with his pants
around his feet and his hand holding camera, and there was naked
girl on her knees with his członek in her mouth.

Of course, they jumped it up. Matthew dropped camera and was
rushing to put his pants back on.

"What do you think you are doing?" I yell on them. Then I point at the girl, who try to cover her shame, and I say, "GET OUTTA MY HOUSE! YOU ARE BANISH!"

Matthew said to let girl get dressed, and that was it. I could not even hear it one word from him. I slapped his face again and again. "You idiot!" I say on him. "This what you do in my house? Bring it little whores?" He covered his face and fell onto couch, trying to hide it himself. I kept hitting and hitting, his arms, his dupa, his head. The girl run outside in her underwear. I said, "Shame on you! Shame on you!"

Then I stopped. Matthew's face was full of blood. I was scared. And then I realize that it was from cut on my thumb. I dropped it shirt. Blood was everywhere.

•

That night I talked to my wife, Agatha. She work in hospital. She wanted to go to Matthew's room, where I ground him, and spank him with wooden spoon. But I said no. The memory of his face with my blood already was kinda bother me. So we decided no dinner for him.

Agatha wanted to know who was that girl. I didn't know. I never saw her before in my life. What they was gonna do with their video? Again, I did not know. Where did they get such an idea? We no had it computer in home, and Matthew was only sixteen!

Agatha walked back and forth. What is happen to our boy? she said. Used to be Matthew liked it church. Allaways he was singing with everyone. Allaways was he on his knees to pray. I remember once he locked it himself in his room, and when he came out he was holding tape he made it of music—"All for Jesus," he was calling it. He had keyboard we gave it to him. I do not like his music, but his heart was in right place. My little boy: I thought he gonna be preacher. If he is failing now, I said to Agatha, is only God's way of giving opening to salvation. Then I get her to sit and bringed it her toast with honey and play for her tape of thunder and rain.

·

Next day at work it was bother me. My father, rest his soul, never had to worry about such things. Me and my brothers never even think to be so bad. Was simpler times then, in Poland after war. We wore it button shirt, nice pants every day. We was calling father "sir." There was no like they having now—you take off your clothes for movie and they giving you award. *Straszny!* I don't know how my father was be managing like this. Now I had to be father. So when Matthew sit at dinner table, I tell to him what Agatha and I decided.

"We are taking you out of that high school. You will go to Christian academy from now on."

Matthew put it down his fork. He was mad, ashame, full of pain. He said we could not do it, he had it friends there.

"That is what I am afraid of," I said. "You will make new friends. Good, Christian ones. When I came to America do you think I had it friends here? I didn't even have it my brothers with me! Still, I came."

Then he said he was sorry for what he did and he promised to do anything. He would never have it girlfriend. He would go to school and come straight home.

"My word is final," I said. "You are going to Christian academy. Is easy drive."

He said it was too expensive and we are crazy.

"We will pay," I said. "Even if I have to work until my hands fall off! That is sacrifice we will make it to keep your brain from rotting inside your head."

He look it on me. But we could not hold it our eyes for long. There was great shame between us—his because of what he did, and mine because I could not find words to say. My father never was talking about such things private with me. When I was young

I was having many girlfriends. Even so, I did not know a woman until I was married—don't tell me I don't know what is it to have it lust in the heart. Still, Matthew should be stronger than evil. So I was ashame of him more than I was ashame for myself. And both shame I could not speak about.

Finally, Matthew said he was not hungry, and he left it on the table his food.

I left it mine, too, even though I am liking meatloaf.

•

Next day I went to store video. I wanted to rent it *Ben-Hur*. I wanted to give it to Matthew so he could know how important is religion, and so I could tell little bit about my life in Poland.

In 1960s, was not easy to be Christian in Poland. We was having Catholic church because the Communists knew it was be very unpopular to ban it. But many other things they ban it—really only you could say you are Catholic and that's it.

But I was not Catholic. I was tailor in little shop in Warszawa, and one day customer gave to me pamphlet telling me how to be saved. Next time that customer came in, I ask him about it. Then he took me to secret meeting in someone's home. There was maybe thirty people. Evangelicals! They talked about how to be free! Of course, you had to talk very carefully. You never could tell who was spy. They was even looking on me kinda suspicious. But I became friends with them. I liked it to be part of that group, to feel there was hope for future.

When I saw it *Ben-Hur* first time, the way they showing believers meeting in secret, and having hope even though the rulers was trying to get rid of them, I became very proud. I don't know how this movie came to be there. I was with group of Christians. We watched it without sound on wall of cafeteria cellar.

Of course, in Poland in 2004 if you want it movie you go get it. Just like where I was living in Ohio. We had it Mustafa Video.

I did not go there much. He is having too many movies with killing and, you know, sexy stuff. It was be so long since I been there that I even forgot about curtain velvet.

I saw it when I picked it up *Ben-Hur*, because he was putting religious movies in back of store. I did not have to look or ask—everybody knows what is behind curtain velvet: porno movies.

I saw Matthew again with that girl on him. I saw kids watching their video, their eyes becoming like jellyfish. I saw in my mind women dancing like strippers, and boys playing with themselfs like monkeys, and tongues hanging out. What is becoming of these boys and girls? How they are learning to treat each other?

I prayed for correct English, and then I say to cashier: "Where is manager?" This poor cashier was very fat hairy young man. He picked it up the phone.

Mustafa came out. He was like man on yacht, with coffee in his hand and shirt unbuttoned so I was seeing his hairy chest. Also, he wore it sandals. He was kinda Arabian, with short black hair combed back like he is Mr. Cool Guy, you know. But he was not that young—maybe in his forties. He look on me with this smile like I was be selling him cookies. His teeth was perfect. He ask what he can do it for me.

I said to him, "Do you think is OK to have it porno movies in store like that?" I pointed to curtain velvet. "Why you are having that here?"

He look it surprised, then he said believe it or not, people rent them.

I said, "But you are having this in store with children's movies! How do you know is no kids going back there? Aren't you ashame to have this with children in your store?"

He said there was allaways someone watching, even on security camera.

"Even so," I said, "you are making so that kids can see it, so that they will want to know what is behind curtain."

He ask if I want him to take it those films out from behind curtain and put where everyone can see. I said no! I wanted him to get rid of those movies! They should not be in store like that, next to children's movies.

He say he appreciate my concern, but he is having other customers who like it those movies. He say is free country.

I said, "Don't tell me about free country. I come from communist country. I know what is it to live there. Believe me, when we were meeting underground, risking our lives, it was not to watch movies with people naked! We wanted to give it something hopeful and good to our children. That was whole reason for coming to America! Not this . . . pornos!"

He ask me where I come from, and I told him. He said he was born in Egypt.

"Then you know," I said, "how important is freedom. We should not use it to rot brains of our children. Is same reason you cannot sell cigarettes to teenagers. You can say is free country, you should be free to sell cigarettes to whomsoever you like it. But no! You cannot harm young people. That is more important."

He drank it his coffee. Then he say he is businessman. Freedom is that he has right to sell and customer has right to buy. That's it.

And I became so angry on him. I slapped it the coffee from his hand. It spilled all over videos there. Then I point finger at him and say, "Are you listen to me? You should be ashame! *Ashame!* You are part of problem! You are spreading sickness with these movies! I will show you! *You* will be one who is ashame!"

He yell on me to leave store.

I dropped it *Ben-Hur.* Then I turn to walk out. In doorway I yell back on him so he know I was meaning business, "*You* will be ashame!"

•

I do not like it to be angry. I never blow it horn. I'm never yelling on dogs that are coming into my yard and leaving poops. God gives us life, and I will rejoice and be glad in it.

But this was different.

There was something in my bones that could not stand it what was happening.

No, on that day, I felt very good to be angry. Never since coming to America did I open my mouth like that.

I thought about how to make Mustafa feel shame. Best way, I realize, was to show him that he is alone, that community did not want his dirty movies. If we come together and make it noise, we could make it change.

When I tell Agatha, she was terrify. She is kinda like woman from time of kings, in those movies where they are wearing big skirts and passing out. She fan her face with her hand. How could you get into argument like that? What do you mean you will go to newspaper? She was asking all these questions like police was coming.

Agatha did not live in Poland. Her parents ran it little shoe factory in Szczecin, but they closed it up during war and went to London, then came on boat to America, where she was born. She never grew up with fear that someone is allaways watching and listening. I didn't know where her fear comes from.

But I remember Poland very well.

One day in 1966 police officers came into tailor shop. I was alone. My knees was shaking. Then comes in old man in dark brown suit. Bald and kinda tall, with glasses with thick black frames. He was having simple tie and shoes, and he smile on me. I knew who it was: Gomułka, First Secretary of the Party! I seen his picture in newspapers.

He say, "Comrade, I am going to very important meeting, and I tore it sleeve on door handle. Can you fix it for me?"

"Yes, comrade," I say, even though I was never Communist. I taked it needle and thread and scissors and I start to work, and he was standing so still, holding arm for me.

Of course, I was nervous. I start to think maybe this was big chance for me. I could stab him between his legs! Or in his throat.

This was before I became Christian, I was having such thoughts. Funny thing was, I did not even care about politics. I just knew I had it chance in front of me. Of course, his guards would kill me right there. But if I kill the First Secretary, maybe it was be new revolution starting. I was be hero in all of Poland! Now! I said to myself. Do it now!

I thought about what it would be like to stab him. How hard for scissors to cut flesh, how blood was be everywhere, on my hand even, and how terrible sound would come from his mouth. Like rusty door opening. Even though I had not read Bible yet, I had it wyczucie—I don't know how to say in English, kinda deep sense—that it was not wrong only to kill in that moment, it was sin.

But sometimes sin is like hole in road that you must drive over, and I thought I gonna have to close my eyes and just do it.

Suddenly, he say, "The eagle is most used symbol of nations. We are all having this symbol."

Then he look on his sleeve, say, "Thank you, comrade," and he left very quickly from shop. I stood still. I thought I gonna make it in my pants. Shop was empty. He left no money for the work.

Can you imagine: Such a quick moment, and I could have changed it history! I was be in all books about Poland. But I simply could not lift it my hand against that one man. I could not kill, and I could not die.

After that, I wore it sunglasses and combed my hair like James Dean—his picture make it the girls crazy—and I told girls that I am personal tailor of Gomułka. Oy, that was big mistake! I was nineteen years old! Years later, there was riots, people begging for bread, and then the Communists thrown Gomułka out; it was over for him. I knew what was be happening after that—once you are put on blacklist, that's it, they gonna erase you from history.

Then friend said to me, "Don't go to shop tomorrow. You told too many stories. They are watching you."

I became panic. What could I say? I am good citizen! I only met Gomułka once! Was only for few minutes, and I even thought about killing him!

But who gonna believe this?

Next day when I turn on street where was shop, I saw man standing next to black car, waiting. He did not see me. My heart was jumping. I went back home. After that, I became convinced that I would be picked it up in black car and sent to prison. All because I fixed it sleeve one day.

That was when I decided to leave Poland and all my family and friends. I went to Catholic priest who was making false papers. After that I took it plane. I arrive in Cleveland in 1971. And I began to learn it English. Was not easy. I learned to make it this sound that is everywhere in it—th, th, th—but still sometimes other things I cannot say it correctly.

Oh, America, with your air conditioning and supermarkets and flag everywhere. I did not think I would end it up here.

•

After church on Sunday I talk with Pastor Hite. He is good man. I like him. I tell him that I want to say something against filthy movies in Mustafa Video. Pastor was nodding and say is big problem. Then he look on me and ask it how to help.

I had it big vision of thousands of people protesting in front of Mustafa, with news cameras putting us on TV. Maybe even we was be getting congressman to speak.

Pastor said let's have it meeting first.

So few days later we have it meeting in church basement. Pastor was there, and so was Bobick, who was police chief and is deacon for us. Pastor from First Baptist was there, and so was pastor from Methodist church. We talked about many things, even things I did not think about. Pastor from Methodist church said to be ready because people gonna say we are against Muslims. I said I don't know Mustafa is Muslim. He is from Egypt and he owns store, that's all I know. Then First Baptist pastor ask if maybe we should have it someone with us with brown skin, you know, to make it easier. I said I am complaining, OK, and is because of my son. I don't care about American skin problems. They say they understand. So then we decide it to write letter to Mustafa to ask him to remove filthy movies from his store because he is dangering kids. We agree to give letter to Mount Zion *Gazette*. After that, we will get many more people to sign it letter to Mustafa. And then ball is rolling, like they say.

I felt very proud. All the pastors was saying I am having courage. Me! Courage!

When I get home from that meeting, Agatha is in kitchen pounding pork chop. I felt so happy then that I try to give her hug. But she spin round and point hammer at me. She say she knows where I was. "Why can't you keep your mouth shut?" she yell on me. "Do you know what will happen if you put it your name and your face where everyone can see it? They gonna send letters here, and phone calls. We gonna have reporters knocking on door! Is that what you want? No peace even in your own home?"

I said, "What you talking about? We are not in phone book. Nobody gonna know where we live."

"They gonna know," Agatha said. "Believe me. You watch: They gonna come knocking on our door. All because you have to use your big mouth."

I said, "Woman, you don't tell me when to use my mouth. God give me words to say, and I will say them!"

"Oh, God give you words," she say, mocking me. "Maybe you should see what your wife thinks before you use them."

I heard it door slam. It was Matthew in his room.

"You see?" Agatha said, pointing. "Already you are causing disturbance! Are you thinking what will be like for him, if people starts talking about what you are doing?"

"He is whole reason for this!" I said. "Him and his friends! Why else I put my name in *Gazette?*"

She turn it back to pork chop and starts pounding. The cabinets was rattling. Even refrigerator was shaking.

Allaways she was making me to feel guilty—about cutting grass, about dishes unwash, about garbage take it out—and I did not like it. I wanted to live in a home, not a prison, and not a circus that my son makes. Like I dreamed about it sitting next to River Wisła when I was not free. Like we dreamed about it together first time we met, at friend's wedding near Cleveland in 1976, smiling at each other when parents give new couple salty bread and plate and glass that they break it. We could hear it everybody singing: *Good health, good cheer, may you live a hundred years. . . .* Who was that girl that sat next to me that night, talking about how beautiful is polka music? And me, was I boy yet or man?

I look on back of Agatha for minute as she pound it.

Then I go to living room and watch it old episode of *Matlock.*

•

Our letter was publish in *Gazette.* It was only small thing in small newspaper, but still I felt proud to see it my name there. Agatha maybe was thinking about my pride, because she did not say anything, even though she was angry. I didn't know if Matthew saw it. He was in his room allaways, playing keyboard, and I did not want to bring him this letter. Someday I thought he gonna see it wisdom of how I am protecting him and others children.

Then reporter call to the house. He say he is having interview with Mustafa, and want to have it interview with those that wrote letter. It was be for news story in *Gazette.* Pastor gave it my phone number to him. It was good thing Agatha was doing laundry. I did not want to have it argument, so I only told her that I am going to church, and that's it.

So I go to church basement. Already there was Bobick and Pastor Hite. We was be the only ones for this interview. Reporter was middle-age white man with kinda floofy gray hair. He wore it glasses and check shirt. He was skinny. He ask why we are trying to have it censorship. And Pastor say is no censorship. Then they argue back and forth like this—is censorship, no is no censorship, yes is censorship, no is no censorship. Pastor ask Bobick to get it dictionary, and he go to office, but when he come back he say is phone call for me: Agatha.

Now I am in trouble, I thought.

But she yell on me that Matthew was missing.

I said, "What you mean he is missing?"

She said he was gone and did not tell her and she was worry and I need to look it for him. Her voice was shaking, she was crying. I became kinda scared.

"I come home," I said. "We look it together."

I thought maybe he run away to this girlfriend house. Or some other friend. Was be necessary to make it phone calls, try to find where they are living. I go back to interview room and explain. Pastor and Bobick said they would come with me to look. I said no, is no big deal, but they insist it. I felt very thankful for that.

But when we went upstairs, we hear it piano music coming from sanctuary. At first, I didn't care. Is church. Allaways they having music. But then pastor said no one else was supposed to be there, so who is playing piano? He said he wanted to check quickly, and he went. We followed. And you not gonna believe it, but it was Matthew. He was playing piano at front of church. We stop there by entry doors. Pastor ask if that was him, and I said yes.

We stand there for a minute. Of course, I was happy that Matthew was not missing. But I was trying to understand what was happening. Was he there for youth meeting? But Pastor just said we supposed to be alone. Was it some kinda lesson? If so, where was teacher? Pastor ask it what was that he was playing. It was sad, slow music, like they used to be playing at funerals. I said I heard it before, but I did not know.

"It's Chopin," said reporter. He was standing behind us now.

"Oh, that's Chopin?" I said. "He is Polish!"

"Yes," reporter say. "But you don't know his music?"

I shrugged, but in that moment I stopped listening to reporter. I realized my son was playing Polish funeral song in our church, and he knew it I was be there. Maybe he even followed me when I left it the house. There was no youth meeting, no lesson.

"Matthew!" I yelled, marching to him. "What are you doing?"

He look on me, and I could not understand it what was in his face. He was kinda surprise, but maybe also angry, maybe also happy. I thought about how strange is my son, playing piano in the church, making sex movies in my home. When he was little, I found him making pee pee on a dead bird in our backyard. I asked him what are you doing. He said he was trying to wake it up the bird. His mind was not allaways going where I could follow. I do not know how he became this way. Now, seeing his face like that, I was little bit embarrass. Pastor, Bobick, and reporter gonna think I have it crazy son, and then they gonna think maybe I am crazy too.

Then he stopped playing and, very calmly, said to me to shut up. Only he used it bad word that I will not use it. We all became quiet. Something about that word and the look on Matthew's face gave me feeling of darkness. I was looking at stranger, and I knew then that there was hatred in my soul. I could not explain it, to feel like that about my son, to feel like that and still love him.

I wanted to turn on those men and say to them to leave it my son alone, go away now, I will handle, but I could not say it, I could not even turn. Their faces gonna say they know that I am bad father who could not even see it this darkness in his son.

Matthew look on me and point at piano and ask it if I knew that he knew how to play. I said yes I knew he was playing. Allaways I hear it his keyboard coming from his room. Then he said did I know he could play Chopin. I said no. He said, "Why not?"

I felt like I walked it into bomb that blows up. I didn't know what to say. I was busy, but I thought that was what he was meaning, that I was busy in the wrong way.

Then he said, "Aren't you sorry?" I did not like it this, the son telling the father what to do. Is not how my father raise me, and is not what Bible say. But it was right thing to do, to make it this problem go away. So I said, "I am sorry. Sorry for putting letter in *Gazette*."

No, Matthew said. That was not it.

"I am sorry," I said, "for making you to go to different school. OK?"

No, Matthew said. There was more. Go deeper, he said.

I was embarrass. But still I look on floor and said, "I am sorry for hitting you."

Matthew said he could not hear me, so I said it again, and there was thing inside me that came apart then.

You are not finish, Matthew said. Go deeper.

I closed my eyes and felt like my insides was escaping out from me. I did not know what Matthew wanted me to say, and also I knew exactly what to say. "I am sorry," I said it over and over again. I could not tell if I was saying out loud anymore. In my heart I was shouting I am sorry, I am sorry that I failed, I failed, and I am sorry, I am sorry, I am sorry . . .

# Virgin Birth

hen I was seventeen I wrote an essay about what happened to me. Here's how it began:

*My name is Marybeth Meczka, and I am a senior at Wallace Toole Senior High School in Mount Zion, Ohio.*

*You might have already heard of me. In the past two weeks, the* Mount Zion *Gazette,* Cleveland *Plain Dealer,* Columbus *Dispatch, and ABC and CBS News in Cleveland and Columbus have all interviewed me.*

*The reason why is that I filed a complaint with my county school board. I had to testify in front of the board. My complaint was that I'm not allowed to have my picture in my senior yearbook. I took my picture with my baby boy, Josh. He's eight months old. In the picture, he smiles like a little gift from God. I won't redo the picture. But obviously*

*I want to be in the yearbook. My school's argument is that the editor doesn't have to print anything he doesn't want.*

All of that is true—I really did put myself out there, chum for media sharks. I'd been encouraged all my life to be a witness for Gospel truth. My beliefs are more complicated now—I can't comprehend my parents' god—but I still believe in truth. I just don't see any point in lying, and I don't care if I upset anyone.

The attention came to nothing, in the end. The yearbook was printed without me in it, and my story faded. I didn't become rich or famous.

Joshie will start kindergarten in the fall. The teachers who don't know his story will judge when they see me drop him off. "Oh," they'll say, politely, clearly having expected an older mom.

The irony is that I probably would've been treated better if I hadn't been raped. (I can hear a chorus of neighbors: *We've shown you love! What are you talking about?* But whose definition of love are we using? And does love make you innocent?) The issue is responsibility. It was one of their boys, and they don't want to admit it. It's easier to pretend it was my fault. Or no one's fault at all.

•

Here's another passage from my essay:

*What I'm really good at is water science. In seventh grade, for a science fair, I explored whether harmful organic contaminants in groundwater, such as pesticides, can be neutralized by combinations of inorganic contaminants, like zinc or manganese. The results were kind of inconclusive, but I won the science fair and got invited to a regional science fair, where I placed first in my age group. I think everyone was impressed with the fact that I thought of the experiment in the first place. (One kid at my school's fair literally just made a baking soda volcano.) I got the idea from an article in* Water Science, *which I begged my dad to get when I was twelve.*

I wrote that paragraph to impress you. Priya, who was my best friend until I got pregnant, told me I was obnoxious, always trying to show I was right, and I have to say I agree.

I learned to brag in church, where accomplishments are signs that your faith is real—and so is God. My parents made sure everyone knew I won a science fair. Pastor Hite announced it from the pulpit.

*Obviously, I'm not Ms. Popular. I really don't get that, how doing well in school is so celebrated when you're younger but by high school it's like the worst thing. Not even other Christians hang out with me. At lunch, if I've sat with anyone, I've sat with the nerds. I'm their queen.*

I didn't understand how to rein myself in, and I didn't know how to make friends. I still don't. I don't know who to blame—my parents? Would I have turned out the same if I'd been born into a different family? Normal kids go to football games, parties, and movies. I shadowed a college professor and did experiments in my basement. Or I went to church. Now that Joshie is getting ready for school I think about how to guide him. I want him to be smart, but I also want him to have friends. It doesn't have to be either/or, but I didn't know that as a kid.

When Joshie turns eighteen, I'll be thirty-four. Say before then I do a part-time bachelor's program. I could have a PhD by forty. It'd be better than working at Target, which is what I do now. My mom quit her receptionist job in an orthodontist's office to help with Joshie. She thought it was only fair that I work, and I'm glad to have a distraction.

•

How do I describe the way I got here? I could make a Venn diagram with Tyler Cousins in one circle and home life in the other, but what's in the intersection?

*I got tired of myself. I mean, boys never looked at me except to make fun of me. Was I allowed to date them? No. But did I still want them to look at me? Yes. Which I struggled with, because I know lust is a sin, but is it also a sin to make others feel it?*

Really, I only did what a lot of girls did.

I became infatuated with Tyler Cousins.

I mean, it was just a silly crush, though of course it felt like so much more. Here's how I described it:

*He delivered the* Gazette. *One day I was out front when he rode up on his bike. Sunlight filled his light brown hair, which was messy and feathery. He had a strong jaw and muscular arms. I didn't know he played football—honest! (He was our quarterback.) He just looked like he could pick me up like a baby. After he tossed a paper at our door I said hi. He lifted his head like a piglet butting its mother's belly and said, "Hey."*

*That night, I checked myself in a mirror. Did my jeans make my butt look too big?*

*I peeked out my window every morning. Sometimes I saw him. I imagined kissing him. Like, we'd sit on a bench by Mount Zion Lake at sunset, and I'd tell him that water covers more than 70 percent of Earth. "You're so amazing," he'd say. "Stars make water when they're born," I'd say.*

My first semester of junior year we were assigned to the same table in study hall. One day he asked if I was taking chemistry. When I answered that I was in AP, he asked for homework help. Whispering, I explained coefficients. He had a small scar, like a white caterpillar, on his tanned left arm. His stomach made noises like whale song. After that, he checked more homework with me. He was the kind of guy other girls were supposed to love, not me. But still. I switched from glasses to contacts and from store brand to Pantene.

Sometimes we chatted. His mom had heart disease. His dad had played football for a small college. He liked to read, so we talked about our favorite books—his was *Hatchet*; I loved *Island of the Blue Dolphins*. Tyler felt he was only getting by. He said I seemed decisive, something he only managed to be on a football field. I said I was sure that wasn't true, which seemed the polite thing to say.

Before winter break, he asked if I was going to a New Year's Eve party at Fatso's. Fatso was Steve Chubb, whom I didn't know. Every New Year's Eve his parents went to a gala in Cleveland and he threw a party at home. I'd never been invited. It was just as well. The Bible forbids associating with nonbelievers, my parents had always warned. But by then, I found solitude too comforting. It felt like a problem. I didn't want to spend all of my time in the basement, and then Tyler Cousins asked me—me!—to come to a party.

I wore a long-sleeved, green-striped maxi dress, plus black leggings and flats. I told my parents I was going to Priya's house. She already had her license, so she picked me up. I'd known Priya since third grade. She was a skinny Indian girl with black hair bobbed at her jawline. More importantly, her dad is a doctor. The sight of her parents' black Audi in our driveway put my dad at ease.

I wish someone had told me (I wish I'd told myself) that I had a right to have fun, that I could stop twisting my fingers as I sat in the passenger seat, heading to the party. I wish I'd told myself to be careful. People aren't out to get you, but they *are* out to get you, you know?

No one noticed when we walked in. (I'd been afraid the party would come to a standstill.) I saw unfamiliar faces. Then I saw David DesRosiers with a beer in each hand, trying to balance a third on his head. It spilled to the floor. Kim Gierek twerked to deafening hip-hop. Ben Bortles ran shirtless through the house, yelling. Everyone laughed. I fought an urge to sneak away.

Fatso, it turned out, was a scrawny white boy with a large nose, droopy eyes, and brown hair parted in the middle. He wore a hemp bracelet and saggy jeans. He pointed us toward beer. When I said I didn't drink, he offered to get me water. I could see why his parents felt him responsible enough to leave alone in the house. So polite, so thoughtful. He scooted through the crowd and returned with a red SOLO cup.

*I had no reason to think anything was wrong. My water tasted like water.*

Priya had a crush on Jeffrey Hildenbrandt from pre-calc. When she saw him in the kitchen she swallowed her nerves and went. I encouraged it, though it left me alone.

*I wandered, looking for Tyler. I went upstairs, which was dark and empty, and saw an open door. It was Chubb's parents' bedroom. Their bed looked like a car under a tarp. There was a flat-screen TV above a fireplace, and a chair next to a dresser. On a nightstand I saw a framed picture of a woman in lingerie—Mrs. Chubb! Who displays pictures of themselves like that?*

*I sat on the bed and thought about hiding for a while. But I had to go back if I wanted to see Tyler. I looked at the picture of Chubb's mom again. It twisted into a whirlpool of colors. A massive sleep was washing over me. The last thing I remember is dropping my water to the floor.*

•

Flunitrazepam, or Rohypnol, which I think was in my water, can knock you out for ten hours, depending on the dose and whether you mix it with alcohol. I wasn't out for that long.

The next thing I remember is Priya shouting. She was beside an open car door. I was in the passenger seat. A brown Count Chocula hung from the rearview mirror. It wasn't her car. To my left I saw Tyler Cousins. His hand was on my shoulder. Priya kept shouting my name. I wanted to break free and be smothered at the same time. My heart was on a skydive, just falling, falling, falling . . .

I don't remember refusing a hospital visit, but Priya later told me I got very angry about it. I remember Priya leading me up the front steps of her house. I don't remember vomiting in her bathroom, or her washing my hair under a warm shower. I don't remember her scrubbing lipstick from my forehead, where someone had written SLUT in cherry lush.

•

I Googled myself. I searched social media. Every day I expected to find pictures.

I didn't tell my parents. I considered myself lucky that they'd been asleep when Priya brought me home.

It seems naïve now, but I thought that was that. I didn't assume the worst. In Tyler's car, I awoke wearing all of my clothes. I wasn't in pain. I wasn't bleeding.

•

After that night, everywhere I went, I felt stares and heard whispers. I told myself to act like nothing had happened: I'd only feel embarrassed if I acted embarrassed. It was a new semester. Everyone had new classes, new distractions. But every time a teacher called my name, I heard snickering. Girls in the bathroom clammed up and looked away. Then I found a note in my locker: "SLUT."

Priya urged me: Tell the principal, confront Chubb, do *something*. I explained my approach, but it sounded lame. High school is governed by a cruel code I was afraid to break, or maybe it's more accurate to say I didn't have the social status to break it.

Tyler stopped by my lunch table. I was alone, reading a book about whales, but I dropped it and put my glasses on. (I'd gone back to glasses.) He asked if I was OK (me: "It just wasn't my best night . . .") and then explained that he'd been late to the party and heard Priya shouting when she found me upstairs. The earnestness in his emerald eyes! He wanted me to know he cared. I wanted him to go away but also never leave. Something stretched from my stomach into my head. Priya told me he'd carried me away from the party, and I thanked him.

"Anyway," he said, "I'm gonna go back to my table."

Those were the last words he ever said to me. We didn't have study hall together anymore. Our brief chat left me giddy, even if he didn't sit with me. He ended up at Eastern Michigan University, where he was a backup wide receiver for a year. Then he joined the Army. According to the *Gazette*, he went to Afghanistan. I don't know where he is now.

•

*I missed my period. Humiliation was one thing, but pregnancy changed everything.*

*I peed on a stick. The result gave me chills. I imagined a freer, smarter, more beautiful version of me who lived in the Caribbean. I really wanted to be that person, instead of the one who now had another human growing inside her. And then I thought about what must have happened when I was knocked out. I became furious and disgusted and terrified. I asked God how He could have possibly let it happen.*

*But then I thought: When Mary found out she would have Jesus did she cry and complain? I'm not saying I thought I was the mother of God. Or that I didn't cry.*

We tell ourselves what we need to hear. For me, that meant deferring to a master plan. If it happened, it was supposed to happen. And yet, I waited a few weeks before telling my parents. For one thing, I could've had a miscarriage, in which case I could've avoided the conversation. But I also needed time to figure out how to tell them.

My dad assembles the M1 Abrams at the Army Tank Plant. He likes to fish and play church league softball, though he says he's gotten too old for both. His black hair is almost gone on top. He likes cheesy action movies. His arms are big enough he could've been in one, fighting Chuck Norris. My mom is meek and effeminate. She respects authority to a fault. She dyes her hair brown, and she's also the pickiest eater. She'll ask a waiter a thousand questions, mostly because she can't have gluten, but also just because.

They were perplexed when I took to science. Occasionally I mistook the question in their eyes—"What is going on with my kid?"—for pride.

I blabbed everything after dinner one night. My mom clasped her hand over her mouth, looking like I was killing a cat on our table. I had to stop twice, but managed to finish without crying.

"Marybeth," my dad said, lost.

"We can go to the police," I offered, "but I really don't know who did it. There were people in that house who don't even go to my school, and it's not like anyone took attendance."

"I'd start with the kid who gave you the water," my dad said.

"Maybe," I admitted.

"And someone must have taken pictures," my dad said.

"True," I said.

"And some kids would talk," he said. "Priya would."

Before I could mention that the thought of making my classmates talk to the police made me want to be buried alive, my mom reached for me. I sat in her lap. She stroked my hair. A clock ticked loudly. I was relieved they weren't angry, or at least not showing it. My mom breathed against me, warm, full of the beef stroganoff we'd just eaten. I'd badly needed a hug.

My dad knelt in front of me and held my hands.

"Sweetie," he said, "we're going to find whoever did this. If God wants him found, he'll be found. But in the meantime, you've been given a great gift . . ."

"That's right, baby," my mom said. She kissed my temple.

"You've been entrusted with a miracle," my dad said. "It's gonna be hard, but you know how Pastor talks about the right path not always being easy?"

I nodded. "Nothing's different about me," I told them. "As far as I'm concerned, in the eyes of God, I'm still a virgin."

I felt calm and right. My dad looked totally flustered. My mom kissed my temple again and burst into tears.

•

I met with Dr. Gianopoulos, an elderly Greek man who talked loud and smooth like a game show host. He ran blood tests. I met with an OB-GYN named Dr. Morrison, a pretty Black lady with a Southern accent. I met with a detective named Dotson who had a Daffy Duck PEZ dispenser in his chest pocket. I met with Pastor Hite. In his office he has pictures of himself on a motorcycle and Elvis bobblehead dolls on his desk. I met with a handsome lawyer named Daniel Cornish. He warned me that unless the police found evidence I had no case. And I spoke on the phone to my brother, Matt, a junior at Liberty at the time. My parents had already told him, so I didn't have to go over the story again. After I told him about Detective Dotson, we talked about PEZ dispensers.

It was a whirlwind, and I was grateful. Without it, the thought of what had happened to me would block everything out. I abandoned the experiments in my basement for the Bible in my bedroom. I needed to feel significant, cared for, assured.

Then Priya and I talked.

She sat across from me on the floor in my room. She'd always wanted to be on *Academic Challenge*, a local quiz show, and she'd finally made it. Her appearance was a week away. And she was knee-deep in college brochures, planning a future that might have included rooming with me, if we ended up at the same school.

"How can you be pregnant?" she asked. "The odds of that happening . . ."

"I know," I said.

"And who would do something like that?" she asked.

"I know," I said.

"And how can you not have a case?"

"There has to be proof," I said.

"But you're pregnant. And I told the police you were drugged."

"But for all they know," I said, repeating what the lawyer told me, "I have a secret boyfriend. For all they know, I'm lying about how this happened."

"But I saw you were drugged," Priya insisted.

"Did you see me get raped?" I asked.

She hadn't, of course. The question thickened the air.

"*Do* you have a secret boyfriend?" Priya asked.

I said, "No!"

"Because someone said they saw you with Tyler Cousins at lunch . . ."

I was surprised and angry: It felt like Priya was putting distance between us. Like I wouldn't have told her about dating Tyler! "I told you: We sat together in study hall. I helped him with homework. That's all."

Priya said, "You would tell me if there was more, right?"

"What actually is wrong with you?" I said. "You were *there* that night."

Hurt, she said, "Yeah, well, not everyone was, so there are going to be rumors."

"Well, that's just the price I have to pay," I snapped.

"What does *that* mean?" she asked.

"People were going to spread rumors anyway when they saw my baby bump."

Priya looked stunned. "You're going to have the baby?"

"Of course," I said.

"Wow," she said. "You think this is punishment. Is that what you meant about the price to pay?"

"No," I said. "Though I should've never gone to that party. What I meant was about other people, not my baby." In truth, I didn't know what I'd meant, or what I was saying. (*My baby*—how quickly I adopted those unbelievable words.)

"But you didn't ask to have a baby," Priya said. "You didn't want this right now."

I shrugged. I felt cornered, numb. A vein popped out from Priya's forehead. She closed the trivia book she'd wanted to study from.

"What about college?" she asked. "What about your career?"

"I don't need a fancy degree to be a good, useful human being."

"So, what, you're going to live with your parents? Work at Walmart?"

Stung, I said, "You know, I wouldn't be in this situation if you'd stayed with me. Was it worth it, flirting with Jeffrey Hildenbrandt? Are you two a couple now?"

I knew they weren't, and I hated that I'd said it. But now I'd broken a seal.

A tendon flexed in her neck. "*You* told me to talk to him, and now you're blaming me? Really? What actually is wrong with *you*?"

"You didn't *have* to go," I yelled. "You could've stayed with me! That's what friends do."

"That's not fair," she said.

"I don't think you know what fairness is," I said.

She gathered her things. "This has always been a thing with you," she said. "You always think you're the smartest, and you're always in people's faces about it, even when you're wrong. It's obnoxious. You wanna have this baby just to show how saintly you are, fine. But don't expect me to kneel down to you."

She left.

Later, she texted me: 'Don't do this. UR smarter than this.'

I didn't respond.

•

On my list of regrets, losing Priya is near the top. I would've loved it if she'd been there, feeling my belly, making me laugh. Or talking me down from panic attacks. I told myself our broken friendship was a sign I was right. My truth was difficult; not everyone would understand. Few are chosen, and so on. Stupidly, I never apologized, and she went off to Johns Hopkins, pre-med. I want to tell her I'm proud of her, but I'm too embarrassed to reach out. She'll probably never come back here anyway. She doesn't need Mount Zion. Or me.

•

*By spring break my belly was showing. The day we came back, walking between classes, a boy pointed and said to his friends, "Holy crap! Is she preggers?" They laughed.*

*I found another note in my locker: "SUCK IT MILF."*

*At lunch, people stared. I knew I had to endure it, and I felt strong, but also I felt ashamed of my hunger. I tried to eat what I would've eaten if I hadn't been pregnant. Eventually I got permission to eat lunch in the library, which helped.*

•

In church, I announced my pregnancy. I didn't want to stop attending, and I couldn't hide what everyone would assume was my sin. If I couldn't prevent rumors at school, at least I could try at church. So, with my parents' blessing, I told Pastor Hite what I wanted. Every service had time for testimony and prayer requests. I would speak then.

Thinking about standing in front of a few hundred neighbors and describing what happened to me made me nauseated, but I couldn't see another way. I wrote a statement and spent days pacing my room, revising, memorizing, practicing. One thing I'd learned from science fairs: Preparation kills nerves.

Then I stood at the front of our two-tiered sanctuary, under studio lights, with a microphone in my shaky hand. Silver-haired Pastor Hite stood next to me in a black suit, his hand on my shoulder. The ceiling had an oculus of blue glass. Glancing up at it, I expected to feel divinely acknowledged. Instead I felt like I spoke from the bottom of a well. "My name is Marybeth Meczka," I began. "I've been saved since I was seven. I want to ask for your prayers, because the Lord has chosen me for the miracle of motherhood. I didn't ask for this, but God is working His will. I will trust in Him, and raise my child in Christ."

Afterward, I cried. People shook my hand. My mother, eyes brimming, hugged me and said, "I'm proud of you, baby."

·

My first panic attack came in the middle of the night that spring, after I felt the baby move. I couldn't breathe. I felt like I was falling through my bed, into darkness. Another time was in a hallway at school. I was taking summer courses. It was July. I was alone. Suddenly I was certain I'd have a SIDS baby, or it would choke and I'd be by myself and not know what to do. I had to lean against a locker and count to twenty. Another time, I was shopping with my mom. She was pitching me a crib, and all I could see was a masked man emerging from shadows, a gleaming knife in his hand.

I'd get panicky when Detective Dotson called. He'd questioned a bunch of guys, but no one said anything. Chubb said he put nothing in my water. People vouched for him. I couldn't tell what Dotson believed. Sometimes he clucked his tongue when I talked.

I'd see boys in the mall and think, *Is it you?*

I'd think, *Will the baby look like him? Will it be hard to love it? Will I be able to look at its face?*

When people said they were praying for me, I'd think, *That's all? Will you be there when the baby comes? If I have to testify in court? When I'm awakened in the middle of the night? When I feel like screaming?*

•

*I was so scared. My toes curled. My throat felt close to bursting. My bowels, too. Doctors encouraged me: "Come on! Push!" And then a sudden release: A little, wrinkled, bloody head appeared in the doctor's hands! There he was, a purple raisin! My shrieking boy . . .*

•

He had pimples and dandruff. It could've been a lot worse.

I fed him from a bottle. I marveled at his skull, watched his blank eyes while he sucked, telling myself I loved him. I know—how could you not love a baby? But my heart just wasn't open to him yet.

I ended my essay four years ago with the yearbook controversy. It hadn't felt wrong to pose with Joshie for my senior picture. As I explained when I confronted the editor (I was suddenly spoiling for fights), the picture represented what high school had been like for me. It was my life. He had no idea what I'd been through. He was just a kid caught in a tough spot, hoping I'd leave the yearbook office. He said my picture promoted unsafe sex and teen pregnancy. Local businesses would pull their ads. The school would lose money.

The kicker is I understood. Part of me did, anyway.

I never sent my essay anywhere. Today, I don't think I'd file a complaint or appear on TV, looking for justice. Mostly I just want to be left alone.

My dad works more overtime, so I don't see him much. My brother transferred to Cleveland State, but he's rarely home. My mom has been more present, though I should say that everyone has been supportive in their own way. (I returned from the hospital to a house filled with blue balloons and a glittery sign in the family room: IT'S A BOY!) We only go out for church. When I tell my mom I don't feel like going she gives me a sympathetic look and says church will be good for me. I'm not sure if she means spiritually or romantically—in her eyes, it's the only place to meet an acceptable man. Usually I relent. I drop Joshie off at the church nursery and sit in the service. I don't look for men. I can't imagine myself with one. I just watch blue light fall from the oculus to the pews. It never looks as pretty as it does in my memories.

I don't know if I'd encourage anyone to do what I did. Joshie is a good boy. He has my curiosity. He wants to see behind things— air vents, the television. It might be a sign of future greatness, or it might get him in trouble, and he doesn't cope well with trouble. He bawls every time he falls. It's heartbreaking, his crying. Still, I don't know.

He's crying now, in the other room. Mom's asleep and he knows me too well to stop, so I better go give him animal crackers. Or, even better, play hide-and-seek. He's bad at hiding—he can't stay quiet or still, and his feet always stick out from under blankets or tables. But it doesn't matter. To win the day, I have to wander around the house, pretending to be deaf and blind, calling out, "Where are you? Where *are* you? . . ."

# Disciples of
# All Nations

---

I am standing in a room in the Iglesia Bautista Libertad in
Mexico City. Support columns, striped green, white, and red,
fill the glaringly lit space. Two dozen boys, ranging in age
from twelve to eighteen, sit in folding chairs, their skin and hair
a mix of browns, blacks, whites, and reds. They watch me. I'm a
white twenty-two-year-old guy from Mount Zion, Ohio, eighteen
hundred miles from here. I've never met actual Mexicans before.
This is my first time abroad.

I've agonized about what to say. For me, speaking is always walking a tightrope, because there are so many words I shouldn't utter.
Like "pussy," for example. My dictionary tells me it was first used in
the 1500s to describe cats; it didn't take on its vulgar meaning until

years later. Does the original meaning win? This is not academic. I've got a roomful of teenagers to connect with. I'll have to explore gray areas, but I don't know if I'll be judged for using salty language, even if I mean "cat" in my heart.

Blessedly, no girls are here, except Jenna, a Spanish major on summer break from Wheaton. She's going to translate. (I don't speak Spanish.) There was a separate, poorly attended session for girls earlier. It's the boys we need to reach. They're at greater risk of getting swallowed by the drug trade. Or so I've been told. I can't claim to be an expert. My knowledge of the country comes from two PBS documentaries about narcos, a book of essays on the politics, history, and culture of Mexico, and the movie *Quinceañera*.

Still, I feel ready. My classes are fresh in my mind (I graduated from Cedarville last month), and, in a sense, I've been preparing for this work all of my life. I trust that I'm right where I'm supposed to be. I have to trust my words are the right ones.

"Can I have two volunteers?"

At first, I think Jenna goofs, because the boys don't react. Maybe they're lingering on the last presentation, a trio of strength trainers—Brett, Ryan, and Ryan—who bent metal pipes and ripped phone books in half. Maybe their parents forced them to come. Or maybe they're just here for free pizza.

Whatever. I pick two kids. They tell me their names: Manuel and Jesús. The latter name I find disrespectful, but that's Catholicism for you. They step hesitantly toward me. Manuel has thin lank black hair in a bowl cut. His eyes bulge as if he's straining to lift a barbell. A stainless steel bull ring pokes through his septum. He is clad in black. Jesús has more meat on his bones. His skin is lighter and freckled, his upper lip adorned with a dark beginner's stache. His blue jeans are fashionably torn, his blue polo shirt unbuttoned. He also has black hair, but it's gelled and spiked. He could be Manuel's brother. They look like they're trying to hide how much they want to know what happens next.

On either side of me is an empty, waist-high garbage bin. Behind me is a faux-wood laminate folding table with two jugs of whole milk on top, one gallon each.

"We're going to have a contest," I say. "This'll be fun."

Jenna says it with gusto.

I offer the milk to Manuel and Jesús, who loop fingers through handles and dangle the jugs near their knees. To Manuel I say, "I want you to pretend your milk is pussy." (I should mention: I didn't warn Jenna, who is a cheerleader type with wavy long gold-brown hair and lightly tanned white skin. Wearing tight dark jeans and the same blue *TBC Mission All-Stars* T-shirt the whole team is wearing, she looks really attractive. The boys are checking her out. I hope she'll fall for me, even though she has a year left at school, I don't know where I'll be in the coming year, and I'm not an athlete.) If Jenna has qualms she doesn't show it (such a pro!), and the boys titter. "Yeah, I know how you talk," I say. "I'm not stupid." Manuel now cradles his milk in both hands. To Jesús I say, "And you pretend your milk is power, completely unlimited power." He nods thoughtfully and then speaks. Jenna translates: "He wants to know if that includes girls." I look at him and nod. "Sí," I say. "As many as you want." He seems satisfied.

Manuel pipes up. "He wants to know why he only gets girls," Jenna says.

He has a point. I've never done this exercise in the Sunday school classes I've taught. In fact, I only recently discovered it online. "That's fair," I say. "Let's say you both have jugs representing power, which includes having as many girls as you want. OK?"

Manuel nods.

Either I've shown flexibility or admitted error. I can't tell from their faces if the boys trust me.

"Now, who wants absolute power more, Manuel or Jesús? Whoever drinks their entire jug the fastest will show they want it most, and will win a very special prize."

Jenna's translation causes Manuel and Jesús to look at their jugs with worry. I want to tell them I drank pool water as a kid—as fun goes, this is pretty clean—but I don't want to plead.

"You guys ready to do this?"

Manuel asks a question. "He wants to know what they'll win," Jenna says.

"Ah," I say, addressing the group, "Manuel wants to know about his reward. Think about how often you do something only because you know you'll get a reward, and yet we know that purity of heart means being selfless. This is what the Reverend Dr. Henry Sturgeon has called 'the heavenly paradox'; the way to get the reward is to act regardless of reward."

The boys stare blankly. I turn to Manuel. "It's a surprise. Anyway, girls are their own reward." Jenna smiles. Someone snorts.

"If you're ready," I continue, "stand next to a garbage bin so you don't spill on the floor."

Manuel and Jesús consider the floor—an off-white, black-speckled laminate (or maybe vinyl?)—then look at each other. They're trapped. Their friends are watching. In a way, this trip has been a big psychology experiment. The ministry website where I got this exercise suggested giving the kids aprons or ponchos, but even without an extra layer Manuel and Jesús get into position. I don't want to emphasize how messy this could be. It might make the tightrope beneath us wobble.

I look at Jenna. "Let's get them to open those caps."

Jenna gives instructions. Like she's starting a drag race, she raises her hands ("¿Están listos?"), pauses, and then swipes down. ("Go!")

The boys chug. Throat muscles piston up and down. Jesús shuts his eyes. Manuel checks his competition. In the crowd, phones have emerged, recording. I see smiles, bright expectant eyes. "Come on, guys!" I shout. "You can do it!" But I don't think they can—difficulty is the point—so I'm not surprised when Manuel's face flushes, milk dribbles down his neck, and he lowers his jug, sloshing milk into the garbage. He gulps air. Jesús, meanwhile, takes smaller mouthfuls. His back arches, his eyes stay shut. Manuel starts drinking again. The strength-team Ryans holler, standing off to the side. Like them, I feel proud of Manuel and Jesús, gamely attacking the challenge. Jesús drools milk from both sides of his mouth. He is concentrating, maybe even praying. They're doing it. They're really doing it. Just then a delivery guy enters the room with a pile of pizza boxes. Brett rushes over to help him. Manuel finally quits, spitting milk into his bin. He has a quart left, but he surrenders the jug to Jenna. Now all eyes turn to Jesús, still chugging, breathing laboriously through his nose. The boys chant: "Je-sús! Je-sús! Je-sús!" I join, pumping my fist. We get louder and more emphatic until, remarkably, with a pained expression and heaving torso, he holds the empty jug upside-down over his bin.

Victory.

The boys clap and laugh. I do, too. Jenna says, "Wow." The Ryans whistle.

Jesús looks like he's about to say something, but all that comes from his mouth is a clean white stream of milk, straight into the garbage bin.

The website had warned about this, but it's still jarring. To me, anyway. The boys say "ohhhhh" like their favorite baller just threw down a vicious dunk. Some laugh. Jesús grips the bin with both hands and retches. Disgusted, Manuel turns away. Jenna covers her mouth. I glance at the pizza guy, who's already left his delivery on a table. He makes the sign of the cross over himself and leaves.

It's perfect.

I wait until Jesús stops vomiting, and then I start preaching. It's the most amazing feeling, words suddenly flowing, anxiety-inducing but also separate from me, like I can listen to myself. "Manuel and Jesús tried to accumulate as much power as they could—all the pussy, cars, houses, influence, all the street cred, *all the things of this world*—and it made them sick. At some point you literally can't take more." Jenna is rapid-fire translating. The boys listen. "What did Jesus say? Easier for a camel to go through the eye of a needle. Think not of your earthly reward. We are in this world, not of it." How many people, I wonder, fantasize about standing before a crowd and verbally letting them have it? Jenna keeps looking at me, impressed. Manuel and Jesús sit down, watching me. "Every human being, at some point in his or her life, has to decide what matters. Everyone is going to have to face his end. If all you want in life is money and girls, all best to you, but it doesn't make the world go round." I wonder what their parents have told them. I wonder if they're in danger *because* of their parents, or friends from school, uncles working for an earthly lord. I mention El Chapo—impossible not to—and his great fortune which caused nothing but misery and darkness. Come this way, I tell them, toward the light. I pray. I tell them anyone who feels moved to make the ultimate invitation, pray the ultimate prayer, can come stand with me, or they can do it at their seat. No one moves. Still, I feel good deep in my bones.

Before I release them to pizza, I fetch from my backpack the special prize Jesús has won: a hardcover Spanish translation of Henry Sturgeon's book, *God of the Godless*, and a pack of Double Stuf Oreos, in case he can make himself drink milk again. Everyone laughs after Jenna translates. Jesús looks at his reward and forces a smile.

•

The website had said to pick two desirable things—why hadn't I seen that each boy should compete for the same thing? Maybe I'd just been too worried about myself. . .

Anyway, I don't want to obsess over a blip. The meeting went well. The proof is that I'm now in a Chevrolet Chevy with Jesús and his friend, José. They're up front. I'm in back. Jesús's window is down, and warm night air blows in my face as we ride through the city. Some buildings are stone intricacies from colonial times, others are all glass and steel. People crowd sidewalks, looking for restaurants or bars, laughing with each other, talking on phones. Except for all the Spanish, it could be Cleveland.

Jenna is at the house of our hosts, a missionary couple who'd picked us up at the airport in a van emblazoned with a crucifixion mural. They claimed they'd unwittingly bought it from a drug lord. They've been in Mexico for six years. But I wish Jenna were here with me, and not just to translate. (Other than explaining about the Chevy—"solo en Mexico"—Jesús hasn't said a word.) Everyone would approve of her—my family, Pastor Hite, my friends. I could see a pleasant future together: kids in the family room, playing with beeping musical toys, Jenna and I in the kitchen, making a turkey cobbler with buttermilk biscuits. Outside, snow drifting softly. So, yes, I have a romantic motive in wanting her around, but I'm ashamed to realize I also want her to see me lay hands on Jesús's friend, whom he's asked me to see. It would make me feel important. Hadn't that been my prideful desire when Jesús approached her while everyone ate pizza and asked her to translate that his friend is sick, and could I come pray over her?

I'd like to think I didn't say yes to feel important. Rather, it's an adventure. There's no danger I could be in that I'm not supposed to be in, so why not go beyond the tourist spots? There's plenty of time for the Zócalo. I want to see how Mexicans live.

I'll admit I'm obsessively good—if you're interested, my senior thesis was about whether I have a choice—which often means boring. I like reading and pondering, and church is good for both. I also like when things fit together just right—which means rules. Advice my mom gave me recently: I shouldn't try to be someone I'm not. Someday I'll meet a girl who'll like what I'm offering. She's out there, she said, and I knew she was thinking about her own life. My dad isn't exactly James Bond—he owns a little furniture store and can balance cups on his belly.

I don't know where Jesús is taking me. The friend we're going to see, who apparently speaks English, has cancer, but what kind and what condition she's in, I'll have to find out. We've passed two hospitals. José attacks the road—fast, jolting, horn blowing. The city seems crowded. I see laundry hanging from windows, a man pushing a shopping cart full of newspapers, a young couple kissing in a liquor store doorway. Our radio blares excited Spanish—is it a sports call-in show?

I've never laid hands on anyone. That's more of a Pentecostal thing. There's nothing wrong with it. Human touch is comforting regardless of whether you've got Holy Spirit flowing through your fingers, and someone in pain might appreciate it. I know I would.

I just hope Jesús doesn't expect me to heal her. I wouldn't presume to try.

I need to pee. I should've gone before I left. I hate imposing on strangers, and now I'll probably have to. The one bit of Spanish I know: Dónde está el baño?

We turn onto a quiet, tree-lined street and stop in front of a yellow building, a two-story cube with curtained windows and a dark door. A black iron fence surrounds it. We get out and Jesús uses an intercom on the front gate, which activates a security light on the house that illuminates everything. The gate buzzes. Jesús opens it and gestures for me to come on.

Here we go. This is what I was called to do.

Behind the opened front door, a girl who looks my age stands barefoot, hiding half her body. She wears a denim skirt and brown spaghetti-strap top. Her brown hair has blond streaks and a pink butterfly clip in it. She doesn't look sick. Jesús speaks Spanish to her and she says to me in English, "Ah, the American. Diana is upstairs."

The living room has a weary-looking couch facing a flat-screen perched on top of a fat old television. The TV provides the only light. On a reddish rug in the middle of the floor are an open black umbrella and a bottle of glue. Jesús talks, patting me on the arm. I look at the girl, who says, "He says he will go up first, make sure she is OK to see you." Now I'm worried it's like an ICU up there.

José sits on the couch, transfixed by the TV. Jesús disappears up a carpeted stairway. I watch the TV for a minute—a telenovela in which a man stares ominously at a woman before a commercial break—and then ask the girl her name. Carla, she says. "Where did you learn English?" I ask. "In school," she says. "Do you speak Spanish?" I tell her I don't, and she hums. "What are you doing with the umbrella?" I ask, but before she can answer, Jesús returns.

The stairway has a brown ukulele mounted on its wall. We climb in darkness. At the top is a hallway lit by a string of holiday lights above a twin-size bed in a room to my right. Primary colors. Give me the right words, I pray. Don't let me mess this up. We pass a bathroom before arriving at a closed door. After knocking, Jesús opens it.

Diana sits on a big puffy white bed, facing us. She has thick black hair that falls to her white T-shirt. She wears pink gym pants and white ankle socks. It feels wrong to notice, but she's really pretty and, you know, well endowed. The room is candlelit, so I can't tell if she's wearing makeup. Flames throw dancing shadows on the ceiling. The room seems better cared for than the rest of the house, from its sleek wood furnishings to its cinnamon smell. Diana smiles, stands, and says, "Hello. You must be the American." I shake her hand and introduce myself, ending with, "I'm here on behalf of Third Baptist Church of Mount Zion, Ohio." She looks like she expects me to kiss her knuckles. (Should I?) Then I hear the door close. I look: Jesús is gone.

Diana asks, "Everything OK?"

"I hope so," I say. Why wouldn't Jesús stay? Is he going to the baño? And I know cancer victims don't always look sickly, but Diana's lips are full and her eyes bright. Her arms appear strong. "Jesús tells me that you're ill?"

There's a struggle in her face, her lips tremble, and then her shoulders drop. She puts a hand on my arm, but can't meet my eyes. "OK, look," she says. "I can't do this. I'm not sick. I know what he told you, but I'm not."

"You don't have cancer?" I say.

"Do you want to sit?" She gestures toward her bed.

"I don't understand," I say.

"You see that?" she says, pointing. In a nook next to the door there is a small black desk with a laptop open on top. I see us on screen. "I was supposed to record you. Record *us*, actually. I was supposed to seduce you." She walks over and slaps the screen down.

"Why?" Inexplicably, my need for the bathroom has disappeared.

She puts her hands on her hips and studies me. "What would you do if I took off all of my clothes right now?"

"Excuse me?"

She raises her voice: "What if I just stripped naked and shook my breasts in your face?"

"I'd ask you to stop, put your clothes back on."

"Would you leave?"

"Probably."

"Like a scared little boy," she sighs. "But you have to admit, part of you wants me to do it. There's a part of you that wants a woman more than you can possibly say." OK, so she's right. I don't know if I'd resist. The only revelatory thing about this is that it's not a revelation. "I know," she continues, "because I let people watch me through that little camera there. They tell me what to do, and mostly I do it. If the desire were not there, I wouldn't make a single peso. It's the same in your country, too."

She looks at me with pity, and I feel like a fool. *Pussy.* On his phone, while everyone ate pizza, what did Jesús text to her? *I'll bring you a dumb American . . .*

"You don't have cancer," I say, angry.

"No," she says. "I'm sorry."

"Excuse me," I say, and open the door.

"He's gone already, I guarantee you," she says.

I look at the bathroom in the hallway: The door is open, the light off.

"Doesn't matter," I say. "I should go."

"What are you going to do—walk back?"

"I'll get a taxi," I say.

"Not out here, you won't."

I grip the doorjamb, grind my teeth.

"I have a car," Diana says. "I'll take you back, no problem. But please stay for tea. I like to speak English. I promise I'll keep my clothes on."

Her smile is wonderful. My anger seeps away. That's part of adulthood, isn't it—controlling anger? Even when you're the butt of the joke? Jesús must have been furious. How could I have not seen it? Had everyone felt the same? Did they humor me with their laughter? I feel a smooth, heavy stone turn over in my stomach, which reminds me of the aching, physical guilt I feel every time I remember an incident from years ago: I'd skipped a rock on Mount Zion Lake, and suddenly a girl popped from under the surface and got pegged in the face. She screamed and cried. My dad, who was there with me, gave me a whipping, and the memory of my stupid act, and the awful feeling it inspires, has never left me. I've never been able to believe that poor girl—or anyone—has forgiven me.

Does Diana know about the milk contest? Maybe she's the one I'm supposed to save—could that be right? Doesn't God work in mysterious ways?

"Do you really film yourself for the internet?"

"On the side," she says, shrugging. "It's good money. Otherwise, I'm a secretary in a bank."

"And Jesús," I say, "he's your boyfriend?"

"No," she laughs. "He's like my little brother. We lived next to each other when we were kids." I nod, though their arrangement is baffling. He brings her men like a pimp? Maybe this, right now, is part of the seduction, getting me to drop my guard. "What about you," she asks, "do you have a girlfriend?"

"Look," I say, "I appreciate that you didn't go through with the prank. It's very nice of you, and I don't know how to thank you. But clearly I messed up here somehow, and I don't feel good, and, if you don't mind, I'd like to get back to my friends. They'll wonder where I am."

"Right," she says, disappointed. "The Baptist church from Ohio. Is that why you came to Mexico—to spread your church?"

I smile at her phrasing. Is it conceited to think she'd try to seduce me for real?

"It's written that we're supposed to make disciples of all nations."

"We already have plenty of Christianity in this country," she says, as if she's tired of having to explain.

"But not the right kind," I say.

"Oh, so *you* know the truth, and you came to bring light for us living in darkness?"

"Something like that," I mutter. She's making me sound pompous. "It's not *my* truth."

She gives me another pitying look. "When do you return to Ohio?"

"In a few days."

She sits on her bed. "Is it nice where you live?"

"Yes, very nice."

"Tell me about it."

"I just finished school, so I haven't found my own place yet."

"And?" she says, luring me in. "Don't stop there."

We all have an internal wall to protect against people we've just met, but for some reason—maybe a combination of the shifting light and cinnamon smell the candles release into the air, her quiet, accented words, my loneliness and fear—mine cracks.

"I'm staying with my parents in the house where I grew up. The neighborhood is not like this—there's more space between houses; green grass; big trees, some of them evergreens. We have a ranch house."

"You have horses?" she asks.

"No, it's not that kind of ranch. It's just, like, the style of the house." She nods, but I'm not sure I've explained. "We have a cat, though, named Uncle Bob. We got him when I was in high school. He scratches people. That's basically it, I guess. It's very quiet. You can go outside at night and not hear anything except bugs. There's a rail line at the other end of town and sometimes you can hear trains. But that's it."

Diana hums, staring at me. "What is it called? I think you said before."

I tell her, and she repeats after me, contemplating the name.

"You live on a mountain?" she asks.

"No. We don't have mountains in Ohio, just farms and shopping malls."

She smiles. I never know what to say about my hometown, which is comforting and indefinable like the candlelight that fills the room. I realize this raises a theological question—if God speaks through me, how can I ever be at a loss for words?

"The town where I grew up is called Tulpetlac," she says. "It's outside the city. There is a hill, and on it, little homes are there like all this concrete garbage. It's not quiet. Even in the night you can hear music and cars and people shouting. I never felt like I slept. And during weekends, there were street festivals. We even had, like, running of bulls, like in Spain?"

I put my hands in my pockets and lean against the doorjamb. Framed photos are on the wall on either side of her bed, but I can't make them out, and hanging on the knob of a closet door is a green scarf, the kind people whip at soccer matches.

"But for me, the most important place was the community center. We went there every day for a tortilla with eggs and rice and beans, and a plastic cup of milk if you were a little kid. I always ate everything. I remember loving that room. I can still see it so clearly. A big square. Two light bulbs hanging from the white ceiling. The walls were white, too, but painted down the middle—a rainbow with smiling children and happy little dogs and blue birds. They made musical notes and words like 'peace' and 'friendship' in big bubbles from their mouths. That is where I learned how to read, in that room. The woman who taught us, we just called her Nana. She was in charge. I can't think of her real name. Maybe I never knew it. But if I close my eyes I can describe her. Maybe you will see her too, if you close your eyes?"

She waits for me. Her voice is mesmerizing. It fills me with a bittersweet feeling, calmness at the center of my body, and I know now I'm not supposed to save her. That's not my role here at all. I'm supposed to close my eyes, and I do.

"Her face was wide and flat, her eyes like little black candies. I remember the lines around her eyes when she smiled, and she had dark sunspots on her cheeks. Her hair was gray and tied in the back so that it fit around her head like a hat. Her eyebrows were so soft and light, like clouds, and silver earrings dangled and shined from her ears like rain. She liked to wear pink, which was still the color of her lips, so very thin. I could see all of her gray teeth when she smiled, straight in a row. I don't know—can you see her? Can you see what I'm describing?"

I feel like I've been pulled gently out of deep water. "Yes," I tell her, and open my eyes. "Yes, I can."

# The Casualty Notice

---

The first dead body I ever saw was a friend of mine, Jean Harper. She'd gone missing. Everyone went out looking for her. My father, too. He figured she'd run into the woods, maybe got caught in a bear trap. We'd played together around the neighborhood, so I knew she was a crier. I imagined it wouldn't take long before someone discovered her bawling behind a tree. This was 1953 and we didn't have a television; we got updates as folks trickled back in. One morning, I went futzing around the neighbors' and found Jean stuffed inside a garbage can behind the Ehrenlicks' shed. I recognized her blond hair. She wore a flower-print summer dress.

I've seen other corpses since then, but the memory of that first one, when I was seven, has never left me. The skin like moldy bread.

The unclean smell. The lifelessness. A puppet the master got tired of playing with.

I lost feeling in my limbs. After, my father scrubbed me under a hot shower until I sobbed.

They never found out who killed Jean. It wasn't the Ehrenlicks; they had a pig in competition at the state fair, where they'd been all that week. The police didn't have all the crime-fighting methods and gizmos we have today.

Anyway, I was a jerk to Jean Harper. That little while that I knew her.

·

I remembered Jean the last time I saw Jeffrey Dickson. He had that bloated emptiness peculiar to the dead, and even in the glare from my flashlight I could tell his skin was ghostly blue. This was 3:30 on a Sunday morning in early August 2006. Two of my guys found him back of the high school on a routine patrol.

I wasn't happy to get the call. The older I got, the more I valued sleep, especially on Sunday mornings, when I typically had to wake early—I was a deacon at the Third Baptist Church. Plus, Mount Zion, Ohio, is just about the safest place you could lay your head, statistically, and I'd had a hand in that. We hadn't had a homicide since before I took over the police in 1996.

They didn't know it was Jeffrey when they called me. My wife, Norma, said it was someone we knew, she just knew it. She had premonitions. Why she couldn't have them about the Pick 6 numbers, I never knew.

"Where's my gun?" I wondered from the bathroom, peeing in the dark.

"I hope you don't sound that confused in front of your men," Norma responded from bed. "And it's in the mud room."

Somehow she always knew where my piece was. (Somehow I always misplaced it.) I sat beside her on the bed and kissed her forehead, which was clayey from a cream. She told me to be careful. I reminded her that I'd once faced a whole jungle full of killers. Unimpressed, and with a motherliness that I found both touching and annoying, she told me to eat something before I went.

When I met Norma, she was dating a Canadian welder. According to her, he called his mom weekly and loved pot roast. He smelled like cigarettes though he didn't smoke, and he never made as big a deal out of Norma's birthday as she would've liked. Norma's like that: There's a princess in her that barely speaks.

Anyway, she got rear-ended in front of a Sears and I got the call. She was driving a big Ford. Five foot three. Brunette, straightened hair. Dark, melty eyes. I didn't know which looked more crushed—her rear bumper or her. I couldn't help it: I offered to buy her coffee. She accepted because she "didn't want to break the law."

It bothered me that she was spoken for. We watched movies with eyes in the backs of our heads, snuck in and out of restaurants like we were stealing spoons. Made me feel powerful in a way I didn't know I needed.

Norma usually knew my needs before I did.

But I'm glad I didn't eat before I saw Jeffrey Dickson that morning.

He had small cuts on his forehead and blood on his lips. Purple bruises on his neck. One eye was half open. A rain shower had fallen a few hours earlier and he was damp. His head was misshapen, like he'd taken a baseball bat to the cranium, and there was blood in his ear. The rest of him was intact. He lay supine under an oak, wearing blue jeans, canvas sneakers, and a white T-shirt with what the kids these days call the "F-slur" written on it in black marker. When I recognized him, I let out a long breath.

"My lord and savior," I said.

"You know him, Chief?" one of my officers said.

I was trying to think of all the codes that needed radioing in, the crime scene protocols, the questions that needed asking. The two officers had their flashlights on the boy, too. Moths landed on him and then fluttered into the murk.

"Knew him," I said. "It's past tense now."

•

What did I know about Jeffrey Dickson? Not much. I feel guilty about that, though no one expected me to befriend teenagers.

He was about five foot ten and beanpole enough that Norma once said we should lure him over for a proper meal. His unruly brown hair added to the impression of grime I got from him in church on Sundays. His clothes were disheveled, his skin pimply. He was a backwoods kid, more at home exploding M-80s out by the railroad tracks. (An officer warned him once.)

And, of course, he was Abe's kid.

What can I say about Abe? He was the kind of guy that, nowadays, people would make a TV show out of. He himself had no TV. He had a wide doughy face pocked with tiny scars and bumps. His silver hair was stringy and fell from an exposed dome to just past his ears. He usually wore a bandana, though, even in church, and a long gray Old Testament beard.

He had owned a lumberyard on the outskirts of town since the early 1990s, arriving just after divorcing his wife, who had refused to join Third Baptist. He kept Jeffrey after she was found passed-out drunk and lying in her own feces on a motel room floor. I knew that much from a handful of conversations with him. I'd see him in the church foyer after service, or in the pews as I passed the offering plate, but that was all. Like everyone, I heard the rumors kids spread—that he fornicated with goats, doused himself in lamb's blood and danced around fires—but I knew better. Or thought I did.

We'd been friends from kindergarten through fourth grade. We'd spent summer afternoons biking around, catching bees and salamanders, dreaming up dumb adventures. When Jean Harper showed up dead he was the only one I talked to about it. He asked all kinds of questions. He sympathized.

When the Dicksons moved, that summer after fourth grade, I never guessed I'd see Abe again. I couldn't have guessed how he'd turn out, either. Scraggly. A refugee from life. I didn't expect him to show up in my church, at any rate. His parents hadn't been religious, whereas my father had been a fundamentalist. But now I thought we'd pick up where we left off: On top of our history, in the great spiritual war, we were now on the same side. Surely, we'd have barbecues and the like. But it just didn't happen. I thought maybe it was because of my job. Or maybe I'd been naïve. I mean, I'd last seen him when Eisenhower was in office, you know? Whatever the reason, I felt shunned. And more hurt than I'd thought possible.

·

Norma wants me to write this. She says when she was a teen she kept a journal, though she hasn't since. I asked once why she kept a journal and she said it helped with her moods. I asked if she'd been depressed since we met, and she said once or twice. Which was news to me. We've been married for thirty-six years.

Obviously, Norma thinks I'm depressed. But look at my life! There's her, and our son, Patrick, who's a lawyer. My first grandkid is on the way. I'm healthy. I just paid off the mortgage on our brown bungalow. I've retired comfortably, which is not something every police officer can say. I've been invited to address the Rotary Club. And when I marched in the Independence Day parade, those twelve years that I was chief, people cheered.

Really, what reason do I have to complain?

I'd say it's just that nothing gets a rise out of me anymore. If I see a kid playing recklessly on a playground, I don't bark orders. I just imagine him smashing his face into a pole. Or any number of emergencies.

•

You have to understand, 2006 was an election year. A lot was on the line. And what this mess with Jeffrey represented (heck, what *Abe* represented) was an image of Mount Zion that my boss, Mayor Wally Toole, had worked to shed. A lot of new houses had gone up on Wally's watch, along with a new recreation center and a whole slew of car dealerships, strip malls, restaurants, you name it. The high school was renovated. Roads expanded; new traffic signs went up. That fall, the big ballot issue was whether to plop a 1.4-million-square-foot mall on forty acres out by the highway. To folks around here, either we were getting too big too fast or we weren't growing fast enough.

The Democratic candidate, Dr. Cherelle Gupta, was skeptical of the mall. Her opponent, Joe Krasko, would've named his children after it. Maybe that's a cruel joke. One of his sons died in '03, and he's an acquaintance from church. Anyway, at the time, Krasko seemed likely to win. I thought how I handled this one case would determine whether I got canned.

I hated politics, but it came with the job. Which was why I went out by myself to tell Abe about his son. It felt like the right thing to do. Also, I felt guilty: His boy died on my watch.

I'd always dreaded having to notify a family about their casualty. I imagined people would see my buzzed gray hair, crooked nose, broad shoulders, and thick mustache, and think of nothing comforting. When I was in Nam, I was sure someone would have to play messenger of death for my parents. I never thought, back then, the part would someday fall to me.

Anyway, I'd never seen Abe's house, which was back of his lumberyard. Heck, it's not like I'd ever invited him over for coffee, either.

Driving there, I felt my gut sloshing and rumbling like a washing machine. I called Norma with the cell phone she'd made me buy. I was always reachable without it, but she'd insisted. When she picked up, I told her who the victim was (she breathed a sigh of relief that embarrassed her later), and where I was going, and said I'd miss church. I didn't tell her about the writing on Jeffrey's shirt, for the same reason I told my men to keep radio silence. The last thing I needed was rumors out there, and I just didn't trust Norma's mouth.

Was Jeffrey gay? I didn't think so. In fact, I'd seen him leaving the movie theater with a girl once, holding her hand. But I knew what would happen if word got out. Both of my potential future bosses would react. Probably they'd want to involve me.

First murder in forever, and it had to be flipping *political*, too.

•

Driving onto Abe's lot, I saw two large barns with stacks of smooth, cut wood, planers, a forklift, and other machines. A gray shed Abe used for an office, a watchful black-and-white cat at the door. It was a big operation. Abe supplied Joe Krasko with most of his lumber, and Joe was the biggest homebuilder in town. I'd seen them backslapping on Sundays, satisfied with their earthly reward.

My tires squelched in the mud as I drove through the lumber-yard, following tire tracks through a clutch of trees to the white ranch where Abe lived. I parked in front of the house. Its gutters were clogged. Weeds sprouted from a stone walkway. The tracks I'd followed led to a blue pickup, its tires caked with mud and a "Dickson's Lumber" decal on the door.

I felt cold, though the sun was already up.

Consarn it, what was friendship anyway? It wasn't like we'd heard each other's voices crack, liked the same girls, or played on the same football field. We didn't serve in Nam together. Abe knew none of my secrets; I knew none of his. All we had were memories from childhood summers and a few conversations decades later. Wasn't that practically nothing?

With a prayer in my head, I killed the engine and exited the car.

Just then, in jeans and a torn, furry bathrobe, Abe opened his door. He had a big black roller case behind him. At the sight of me, he stood straight and put his hand on his heart. I was startled, too.

"Going somewhere?" I said.

"I was just about to call you, Ken."

"Is that right?" I said. Abe had rings under his eyes and a sweaty forehead. His pecs sagged like turkey wattles.

"I can't find my boy," he said. "He didn't come home last night."

"I know," I said, approaching. "That's why I'm here. We found him."

"You did?" Abe said, looking at my cruiser. "Where is he?"

"We found him out at the high school."

Abe looked ready to launch into a tirade until he saw the look in my eyes. "Is he all right?" he asked.

I shook my head. The washing machine rumbling inside me stopped dead. I told him.

Abe's face constricted, his eyes boring into mine. Then he looked away and said, "Oh." He sat in his doorway, repeating, "Oh."

It looked like an animal was trying to spring from his mouth. I imagined how I would've felt if someone had told me Patrick was gone: like I was standing at the edge of an abyss in pure dark.

"How?" Abe asked.

"Looks like he was beat up pretty bad," I answered. "Maybe strangled."

Abe covered his face and cried. I looked inside the house. Abe's luggage was thigh high. Further inside I saw a rocking chair on its side and a glass tumbler on the carpet, surrounded by muddy footprints. What is this mess, I wondered, and where was he going?

"Abe," I said, "you wanna go inside, sit for a bit? I know it's hard, but I gotta ask questions."

"I need air," Abe said, heaving. "I just need some air . . ."

"You been out already this morning?"

Abe said, "I've been here all night."

"I saw tracks," I continued, "and mud on your tires. Looks like someone's been driving your truck . . ."

"Oh," Abe said. "No, I went out searching an hour ago. Thought maybe I'd see him somewhere . . ."

I nodded. "When's the last time you saw him?"

Abe closed his eyes and scratched his beard. "Last night," he said. "He was here last night, just before midnight, I guess."

"Did he say anything that might make you think he was in trouble?"

Abe looked down at his hands. "No," he said.

"Had he *ever* been in trouble? At school or anything?"

"How do you mean?" Abe asked.

I shrugged. "Did he have any problems with anybody?"

"The kids picked on him some, I guess," Abe said.

"What kids? You know their names?"

Abe wiped his eyes. "No. Just some kids who didn't like him. I don't know why." He cried some more before adding, "Who knows how they're running these schools nowadays! It's not like when we were growing up. You remember?"

"Yeah," I said.

"Remember that time I beat Andrew McGee in that race around the school?" Abe said. "Whole class saw it."

"He went on to be a track star in high school," I said. "Broke a record or two."

Abe smiled and nodded. "Beat him by a mile," he said.

The words hung in the air, lonely and sad. I thought this diversion odd, but people will grasp at comfort wherever they can find it, I guessed.

"Going on a trip?" I asked.

Abe glanced at the luggage. "Ah, you know," he said. "I was just moving some stuff to the office."

"Must've been at it all night, if you're anything like me," I said.

"Yeah, I was . . ." Abe began, but sniffled and trailed off.

"I see your chair got knocked around in there," I said. "How'd that happen?"

"I just tripped," Abe said. "I'm always falling over that thing."

I knew he was lying. About what, I didn't know yet. Maybe, when Jeffrey didn't come home, Abe knew we'd come calling and was hurrying to hide something; maybe his luggage was full of illegal weapons. Maybe a feud with a neighbor or relative had claimed Jeffrey and now Abe was fleeing before he got it next. All I knew was that you wouldn't trip over a chair and leave it like that unless you were indisposed or in a hurry.

I had to get into the house. It's a decision I've been thinking about ever since.

"Well, you gotta be careful," I said. "Maybe you ought to move it."

"Been meaning to," Abe muttered. His hands shook.

"Abe, we're gonna find whoever did this. I want you to know that. I've got my best people going over the scene. The school has surveillance cameras and we're looking at the tapes. The coroner's a Case Western guy, smart as a whip. Believe me, if the killer so much as flicked dandruff from his shoulder, we will find it. Just a matter of time."

Abe buried his face in his hands. "My boy!" he cried. "I can't believe my boy is gone!"

I stood there for a minute. My mind drifted to Norma. I wished I was in bed, listening to her breathe, watching sunlight fill our room. I imagined removing Norma's nightgown, kissing her shoulders and back. I hadn't seen her naked in years. God's rule, not mine. I thought the longing was something I'd get used to. But I never did.

"Abe," I said, "why don't we go inside, get a glass of water. Maybe we can pray together."

"You wanna come inside?" he asked, incredulous.

"Yeah. Maybe I could take a look in Jeffrey's room, you know, in case there's something helpful. Maybe he kept a journal. I don't know."

"Right now?" Abe asked. "I mean, it's not really clean. And I kind of just need to be alone, I think."

"I know it's hard," I said. "But every moment we wait, whoever did this gets farther away, and as bad as you feel now, I *know* you won't wanna feel like justice was never done on this. So, in a few minutes, after you've had your water and I've taken a look in his room, I'm gonna call another unit to come and collect evidence—Jeffrey's papers, his photos, his computer or cell phone if he had them—anything that could help. And you and I are gonna go identify him."

Abe looked confused. "Identify him?"

"It's standard procedure," I said. "We need someone to confirm his identity."

"Well, then, let's leave right now," he said, standing. "I don't need any water. I'm going in your car?"

"Hold on," I said. "I'd still like to take a peek in his room, if you don't mind."

"I thought you said someone else was coming for that," Abe said.

"I'm here now," I said, "and if there's something helpful, I'd rather find it now than later."

Abe looked desperate. "I thought you all needed a warrant before you could come in someone's house."

Something jiggered in my throat. "No, not really. Why, is something wrong?"

"No," Abe said. "I just. . . . The thing is, there's nothing there. I wouldn't want you to waste your time. If you wanna take me where you need to take me, I'm ready to go."

"What do you mean there's nothing? It's where he stayed, isn't it?"

"Yeah," Abe said. "But I mean it's just his bed and clothes and schoolbooks and stuff."

I said, "When he left last night, did he drive? Was he picked up? Did he walk?"

"Why?" Abe asked.

"Well, for one thing," I said, "if he was with anyone, I wanna talk to them. And for another, we didn't find his wallet. Maybe it's in his room. You see?"

Abe said, "I'm sorry, Ken. I guess I just have a hard time trusting authority, you know?"

I said, "This ain't authority, Abe. It's me. I'm just trying to help. If you're worried about pictures of naked girls on his walls or something . . ."

"No, no," Abe said. "It's not that." He laughed. "I guess I'm just feeling a little weird, you know. All this is suddenly happening. I just wanna get this over with, the identifying. I just wanna see my boy . . ." He sat in his doorway again.

Oh, brother, I thought. I hadn't expected to be this long. Heck, I thought, maybe I *could* let someone else search the house. I didn't know why I always had to be the guy. But I guess that's what got me my job.

"I'm just gonna be a minute, Abe," I said. "I'm just gonna check about that wallet, maybe see if he wrote a name or number somewhere. It could be important."

Abe looked up. "You're not gonna let me be, are you?"

"I came here as a courtesy," I said, "to let you know I'm handling this personally. And I *am* gonna handle it. You just gotta let me do my job."

After swallowing hard, Abe said, "OK." He stood and let me enter the house.

I kept replaying his "OK," trying to read into it. It rubbed me wrong.

The front door opened onto Abe's living room, carpeted the color of beach sand. Aside from the overturned rocking chair and glass tumbler on the carpet, the first thing I noticed was a crater in the wall beside the rocker, and below it, near the floor, a splotch of red that had been half-heartedly wiped. Like someone had had his head put through the wall. I had the same queasy feeling I'd had, all those years ago, finding Jean in the Ehrenlicks' garbage can.

I don't know how I didn't hear Abe cock his gun. Or, frankly, how I couldn't tell he had one. People usually give it away somehow. I'd like to say another sound distracted me, but it's not true. I was just sloppy.

The bullet burst through my right thigh with a scarlet spray. My ears rang; the shot echoed from the walls. I twisted, saw blood dripping down my leg, and fell.

"I'm sorry, Ken!" Abe said.

He pointed a silver snub-nosed pistol at me. Black shapes spread across my vision. My leg felt molten.

"I'm not gonna kill you," Abe continued hysterically. "I just need to get out of here. You're gonna be all right. I just need to get out of here . . ."

I squeezed my eyes shut. When I opened them again the black shapes were gone.

"What are you doing?" I shouted.

"I didn't mean for all this!" Abe pleaded. "I'm not a bad person! You know me, Ken! I'm not a bad person!"

"You killed your boy?"

"He was stealing my money!" Abe cried, seething. "For drugs!"

I barely heard him. I pressed my thigh. Was my artery severed? I needed to stop the bleeding.

"He started choking me," Abe went on, using his gun hand to wipe his eyes. "I confronted him and he started choking me. You believe that?" He wept. "My own son!"

I kept repeating "Please God" in my head. I envisioned Abe pointing his pistol at my face and firing. There was no way I'd get my gun out in time. I was too shaky.

"What are you gonna do?" I asked.

"I'm getting out of here," Abe said. "Going far away. I'm not gonna hurt anybody anymore."

"You won't get far," I told him. "Everyone's gonna come after you."

"Yeah," Abe said, "I know. I didn't think you'd find him so

quick . . ." He lowered his eyes. "Gimme your car keys."

Defeated, I pulled out my keys and tossed them over.

"I'm sorry, Ken. I didn't mean for any of this. Pray for me?"

Abe backed up, gun pointed, and dragged his luggage outside.

I heard the case's wheels scraping Abe's walkway pavers.

I looked at the blood oozing from my leg. I felt dumb and betrayed and frenzied and scared. My brain issued commands I couldn't follow: Grab your radio, shout the right orders, find a towel, stop the bleeding. Somewhere in my mind was an image of Norma and Patrick dressed in black, having coffee and biscotti in a roomful of mourners. I heard rifle fire—a sound lodged in my memory since Vietnam. I was enormously thirsty.

I pulled out my gun and got onto my stomach.

Belly-crawling to the door, willing myself not to pass out, I was filled with anger.

At the doorway, I saw Abe stuffing his roller case into the back-seat of my cruiser, fifteen yards away, the snub-nose still in his hand. I raised my pistol, steadied myself as best I could. As he reached for the driver's door handle, he saw me and froze.

My shot punched through his left leg. He hopped, groaned, looked in disbelief at the crimson stain spreading on his jeans. Then he pointed his gun at me and fired.

I squeezed and squeezed, hitting Abe in the chest as he fell, before I lowered my head. Bullets passed over me, exploded in the doorframe. I heard the casings' ricochet and the hellish bursting of rounds from my own weapon. The ruckus was loud enough that I couldn't hear the scream coming from my mouth until my gun had nothing left and I looked up and saw Abe lying in the mud. I kept pressing my trigger. And then I stopped yelling.

•

Once or twice a year I visit Mount Zion Cemetery, always after Sunday service. Pastor said it'd be good for me, and anyway, I like the cemetery. Jeffrey and Abe's section is called The Garden of Peace. There's usually a fresh mound somewhere in the verdant lawn. Joe Krasko's son is buried there, too—Joe's there every time. We nod at each other. To a lot of people's surprise, he lost the election in '06, and the mall he wanted so badly got built anyway, after the developer threatened to sue.

As far as I know, there are no Dicksons left in the area, but every time I've visited there have been flowers at Jeffrey's grave. Carmine peonies. Violet geraniums. It's nice to see. The marker identifies him as "Beloved Son." A vase is hidden in Abe's limestone marker, which memorializes him as "Beloved Father and Son." Nobody leaves flowers for him.

I'm still mad at him, even though I feel bad for him. I should've invited him over for coffee. But I guess I'd wanted to shed him, too.

I keep seeing his shocked look when he saw my gun pointed at him. And if I'm honest, part of me is glad I pulled the trigger. I hate that about myself.

Norma said, when I was recovering, that I knew what the job was when I signed on. She was trying to prop me up. But it's been almost four years since I turned in my badge, and I still don't know what the job was. Why? Because I don't know how I came to be out there that day, pulling a trigger on Abe.

From the cemetery, my drive home takes me past what is now Wallace A. Toole Senior High School. They named it for Wally after he died. In front is a great red buckeye tree that was planted in Jeffrey's memory. It's beautiful. I remember the dedication. About three hundred people came, including reporters. Word had gotten out about the writing on Jeffrey's shirt, and the media picked it up. Suddenly, we were a Podunk town again. I didn't say anything about drugs. I never found proof, and not for lack of trying.

Do you understand? I don't know what happened. I don't know why Jeffrey died. I don't have answers for those questions, and with Abe gone, I will never have answers. All I can say about what happened is that it was ugly and evil, and that doesn't feel good enough, to have to use empty generalities about life or human nature. Was that my job—solving evil? Understanding what can't be understood?

This bothers me more than I can say.

Times are changing; that's what I said when I told Norma I was retiring. "That's silly," she said. "Times are *always* changing." "Well, then maybe it's me," I said. I didn't like the apprehension I felt every time I walked through a doorway. I got tired of keeping track of my gun, even at home. No more guns, I decided. No more politics. No more dead bodies. All of it bothers me more than I can say.

# Father's Day Sermon

---

**T**o my father, I never stopped being twelve years old, an important age for me—I'll tell you why in a minute. We've all felt the frustration of visiting home only to travel, against our will, back to childhood. Parents, don't pretend you're innocent. My father would ask if I wanted a snack. He'd offer to teach me how to warm up food. He would give me the remote control with "you can watch your cartoons now." If I left the room he wanted to know where I was going. It was little things like that. I thought I'd led him to believe I was immature, incapable. Eventually, I realized he didn't know how to treat me like an adult because, in some fundamental way, and despite his age, *he* was not an adult.

Jesus said, "Anyone who will not receive the kingdom of God like a little child will never enter it." But I don't think my father was simply trying to earn a ticket to heaven. And I've never read that verse as an invitation to arrest your development, though my father might have.

The first truly adult conversation I had with my father was when he asked me to end his life. He was on his deathbed, you see, in a great deal of pain. His cancer had spread everywhere. He chose to play out his final scene at home, but the comfort of lying in his own bed couldn't ease his pain. Nor could any dose of medicine. Nor could prayer. Nor could my presence at his bedside.

Do you remember the worst physical pain you've ever experienced? Maybe you took a bullet in a war. Maybe you were in a car accident. For me, it was a shot a doctor gave me once beneath my fingernail. I'd gotten a splinter under the nail of my ring finger, and the doctor, wanting to remove it without violating the Geneva Convention against torture, needed to numb the nail bed. The shot was so intense I asked afterward if I could leave a small memorial, like my initials engraved in a cabinet or the date scratched into the exam table.

The point is, no matter what you or I have experienced, it doesn't compare to the physical pain my father felt all day, every day, as his body turned against him. I could barely bring myself to visit. His skin was gray and chafed and looked shrink-wrapped to his bones. His fingernails were yellow. I was frankly repulsed by the sight of his black tongue, like an eel in his mouth. Sores and bruises appeared on his flesh. He convulsed and shivered and sometimes whimpered and cried. Some days he looked straight through me, like he didn't recognize me.

Don't let me suffer like this, he pleaded one day. Don't let it go on.

Normally I try to save souls, but my father was begging me to release his. All it would take was an overdose of morphine. He could even administer it himself—all I'd have to do was provide it.

I was surprised, of course, both at my father—who had always been a Gibraltar of Christian faith—and at myself—because I couldn't respond. You might be thinking: Ted, this was an easy call! Remember your faith, your training! And the answer was already in front of me: It's not for me to decide who lives or dies. I shouldn't presume. I should let the master plan unfold. But every time I reached for that answer it slipped through my fingers. I groped in the dark.

Remember your faith. Remember your training.

Instead, I remembered being twelve years old.

Except for my father and my wife, I've never told anyone this story, and I know some of you might think there is nothing extraordinary about it—it's yet another tale of drama between a father and son. The story most of us believe to be the most important, after all—the one that came to be known as the greatest ever told—is about a father and son. I can't claim to top it. This one is important to me simply because it's mine, and I think you have a right to know who stands in this pulpit every Sunday.

When I was twelve, Mount Zion was not the booming metropolis we know and love today. There was no Northview Shopping Center, no big-box retailers on Route 20, no as-seen-on-TV car dealerships, none of the housing developments that eventually sprang up with rec centers and man-made ponds. There was an old public square with a gazebo and a house whose claim to fame was its spot on the Underground Railroad. And there was our church, Third Baptist. It was a different building then. My father brought us every Sunday. I used to sit toward the back, on the right side. I remember listening to a young Pastor Virgil—some of you remember his fiery sermons.

I've been coming to Third Baptist since I was born. Actually, my earliest memory is of Joseph vomiting on the Baby Jesus at the church's Christmas musical. He'd had a stomach virus that year. Pastor Virgil rushed the stage and wiped the Baby Jesus doll with his necktie. He then brandished the doll to the audience and declared the devil couldn't stop the show. It was funny. Everyone was brash then, I guess.

When I was twelve, my Sunday school teacher was a man named Ron Horvath. Most Sundays he wore khaki slacks and a dress shirt with the sleeves rolled, showing off his muscly arms. In colder months, he sported a red letterman's jacket with LORD'S GYM across the back. He had spiked black hair, a tree-trunk neck, and sun-browned skin even in the winter. A gold wedding band squeezed his finger. At the high school, he was the wrestling coach, which made me wary—I thought he might try to recruit me, but no amount of persuasion would get my skinny shanks into a unitard in front of girls. And his honesty kept me on edge. One Sunday he confessed he'd lost his virginity in high school. Then he admitted to touching himself at the same age. He was telling us about converting from a life of sin, and all of this was before he was born again, was the point.

Normally I clammed up in class, believing the nitpicky observations I made about others would likely be made about me if I opened my mouth. But demonstrating that you were thinking about the lesson would score points with the teacher—kids everywhere, of every age, know this—and I wanted to earn enough to coast until Easter. So when Ron asked us to imagine the enormity of Jesus— God in the flesh—dying for our sins, I raised my hand.

"How was it possible for Jesus to die if he's God?" I asked. I gave myself a mental pat on the back. A fine question! Thoughtful. *Theological*, even. Ron tried to parse physical versus spiritual, but it only got me wondering if there were, in fact, *two* Jesuses, which was not what he was trying to say. Then I observed that God shouldn't even be able to feel discomfort, and that really got Ron in a huff. I didn't know I'd stumbled into a classic brainteaser Christians have been debating since forever. It just felt like the movie of my life was dissolving into a bubbly, burned ribbon of celluloid. The divinity of the wind. Reality set in: I was going back to Ron's class. Nothing further would be done.

That'll be that.

And I did go back. Ron waited to apologize until after class, after everyone had left. He told me to stand in front of him. Nervously, I did. I couldn't look at his face. He could barely get the words out. Then he gave me a bear hug and, while I tried to swallow my pulse, he told me he loved me. After that, he let me go, and the incident was never mentioned again.

Did you know you can be bothered by something without realizing it? Some call this the subconscious. I prefer to believe our souls carry on a silent communion with God, and this must shape us when we're unaware. However you want to think about it, the fact is this episode haunted my teenage years, though on the surface I'd dismissed it, filed it away, told myself that I had, in fact, been in the wrong.

Proverbs 20:30: "Blows that wound cleanse away evil; strokes make clean the innermost parts."

And later, in the twenty-third chapter of Proverbs, we find: "Do not withhold discipline from a child; if you strike him with a rod, he will not die. If you strike him with the rod, you will save his soul from hell."

But you know something is wrong when you turn down all invitations from friends, when you're angry with everyone and everything, when you sneak out at night to spite your parents, when you start drinking to feel less alone, when you contemplate plowing your car into telephone poles. You know something is wrong when in college you seek out only the books and art and people that confirm your bitterness, when you convince yourself that sarcasm is a good way to relate to people, when you shake the dust of your upbringing from your shoes as you run away.

You know something is wrong when, at the age of twenty-two, you hear that Ron Horvath is to have a plaque hung in the high

Jesus was a central pillar of my worldview, and suddenly it couldn't hold weight.

Well, Ron didn't have much patience for me. He told me to stay after class, so I stayed. He straightened chairs and pocketed a nickel from the floor as he followed the last kid to leave, closing the door after him. Then he stood in front of me, fists on hips.

"Were you really confused or just being a jerk?" he asked.

He had hazel eyes and a jaw that could crush a soda can, shaved smooth like a soldier's. "I'm not a jerk," I said. I resented it when people assumed the worst about me. I was, in fact, pathetically good.

"So then what?" Ron asked. "You think Jesus didn't actually die on the cross? You think it's all some practical joke?" He pointed at me. "You need to be very careful about what you're saying. You're in God's house."

"I'm just asking," I said. "God doesn't allow questions?"

"Not your kind," Ron said. "Don't you realize what you said? What's gotten into you? Committing blasphemy in church! Aren't you ashamed of yourself?"

Truth is, I *was* a little ashamed, but I also felt—and still feel—that it's OK to ask questions, especially if you're a kid. So: I insisted I was just asking out of curiosity, but Ron said that Satan had gotten his claws into me. Well, that stung, and I said something I probably shouldn't have: "You're mad because you can't answer my questions. I don't think you know how."

A condescending thing for a twelve-year-old to say, I know. Ron said I owed him an apology. I asked what for, and he said for insulting him and the Lord in his class. My conscience urged me to take the plea bargain—I'd never confronted an adult before, not even my parents, and this was goosebump-raising, mouth-drying territory. An apology would've given me a green light to get out of there. But no, I couldn't do it. I felt I was right—about my questions and Ron's inability to answer them.

This didn't please Ron at all. "Apologize!" he ordered.

I told him I hadn't done anything wrong.

"You will apologize right now," he said, "or you *will* be sorry!"

I stuck to my guns, and after arguing some more he grabbed my arm and had me place my hands on a chalkboard at the front of the room, like a criminal waiting for a pat down. When I tried to turn, he grabbed my shirt and, in one swift motion, yanked it up over my head, exposing my bare back. Then he removed his leather belt and gave me a lesson I never forgot.

The first blow landed like a hot surprise. I thought it wasn't so bad, actually. I'd gotten worse at home.

Then the second blow landed. And the third. Then many more—I lost count. Each blow was harder than the last, the belt giving a sharp crack as it broke air with his final swing.

I trembled, boiling all over. I thought I felt blood running down my back, but I ran my hand back there and it was dry.

Ron said: "That was nothing. Remember that the next time you think Jesus didn't feel any pain. That was literally *nothing* compared to what He suffered. For *you.*"

Standing there, pain pumping through me, I thought he was right. I felt stupid and small and ungrateful and guilty.

I said nothing to my parents. During the service afterward, I leaned forward to avoid putting pressure on my back, and kept a constant watch for Ron. At home, I shut myself in my room, and if my father hadn't opened my door just as I was changing my shirt, he might never have seen my welts, and the whole episode might have remained secret, because I don't think Ron would've told unless he had to. But my father did see. He asked about my back, and I couldn't help it: The truth blubbered out of me.

Now, this is the crucial part. Reaction is just as important as disruption. I was too young to know about child abuse. It was not something spoken about, at least not where I was listening. Nor could I have explained how Ron had crossed a line. To a twelve-year-old boy, a lot of adult behavior is inexplicable. My father, on the other hand, *should* have known, even though he was raised in time and place in which getting a whack from your teacher—rule to knuckles, paddle to backside—was accepted. He was, after al equipped with the words Jesus spoke in the Gospel of Matthew that "whatever you have done to the least of my brethren, you hav done also unto me." So after he heard my story and clenched hi jaw and said, "I'll take care of this," I felt relieved. A grown-up wa on my side.

What I couldn't have realized was that I'd placed a balance in hi hands, if you will, with me on one scale and our church on the othe Even Ron's resignation as a Sunday school teacher would've raise eyebrows. Questions would've been asked. Maybe he would've con fessed to a friend, or his wife might've spilled the secret, and the the rumor mill would've churned. Other parents would've grow concerned. Ron's livelihood at the high school could've been endan gered, and any publicity would've been bad for the church.

A few days passed. My father was never imposing, though he' always worked in construction or with heavy machinery, but I sti worried he'd go *mano a mano* with Ron—a fight he would surel lose. Ron had been a linebacker and wrestler; aggression was his spe cialty. But I figured that's how *I* would've handled things, so proba bly any day my father would come home bloodied and bruised. C course, he didn't. Before the week was through, he visited my roor and the only marks on him were grease stains on his work shirt.

He said, "Son, I had a talk with the pastor, and he spoke to yor teacher. When you go to class on Sunday, he's going to apologiz And that'll be that."

Now, I'd already had a taste of what arguing with an adult cou get me, and anyway, you could say that my ability to recognize tl paths before us was as limited as my father's—it wasn't until lat for example, that I realized we could've simply joined a differe church. Also, one of the Ten Commandments is to obey your pe ents. So the resistance I offered that day was like a whisper ir school to commemorate his retirement, and you become so enraged that, during a visit home for Christmas, you set the school on fire.

Yes, it's a mystery no more. It was me, some forty years ago now.

I didn't set out to burn the building. I didn't tell myself I was going to do that. I went in the middle of the night to look at the place where I'd felt so much anguish. This was years before everyone had surveillance cameras and fancy security systems. The school wasn't protected that way. So I thought I might scratch some words into doors. Maybe, at worst, I'd throw a rock through a window. But as I turned one corner, I saw an open window. I'd begun smoking in college, so I always had a lighter in my pocket. I fit my arm into the opening and lighted the space: a supply closet full of mops, containers, and tools. I crawled in.

As I said, I hadn't made a decision to set a fire. At least not until, standing in that janitor's closet, I saw cans of WD-40, and then the devil got hold of me for real.

I'm so ashamed. I'm so ashamed . . .

I want to say I experienced an orderly progression of memories and emotions that ended in fire. But what I discovered was that, though I hadn't told myself anything about it, though I hadn't consciously decided it, I'd known before I stepped out my door that night that I was going to burn the school down. I'd never fantasized or joked about it to anyone. I'd never given it serious thought. But, somehow, I'd known it for years. It was like waking up to realize I'd always been steeped in fire.

I began in the athletic offices. Their wooden doors were locked; I sprayed them and applied a flame. When a fire burst up, orange and bright and hot, I felt exhilarated. It had worked! I was actually doing it! I set two more doors ablaze and saw flames burning through the ceiling before I turned and ran. In the unlit hallway I heard the fire alarm and saw flashing white lights. I expected sprinklers to jump to life, but they didn't. I read in the paper afterward that the system was faulty, but in the moment, I was surprised. I stopped at the library, where I sprayed under the locked doors. The space was carpeted. Soon it, too, was on fire. My last stop was the administration office, which I lit the same way I lit the library. Then I crawled back out the window in the supply closet, sprayed what was left of the WD-40 over the containers of cleaner and bleach there, and stretched to set it alight.

I remember seeing steamy breaths leaving me, aglow from the flames. My side cramped, and my hands stung where I'd burned them. But I felt—I don't know how else to put it—fulfilled. Like I'd finally met myself.

Eventually, I heard sirens. It had begun to snow, just a few tiny flakes. I ran as fast as I could, keeping to the woods or people's backyards. At that hour, no one saw me, not even my parents, who were sound asleep when I tiptoed back into our house.

You've heard me speak about the devastating power of shame and guilt. The Bible gives a most eloquent description of those who walk in the way of Cain: waterless clouds, swept along by winds; fruitless trees in late autumn, twice dead, uprooted; wild waves of the sea, casting up the foam of their own shame; wandering stars, for whom the gloom of utter darkness has been reserved forever.

Well, I didn't wander in darkness for *that* long, in part because I told myself it wasn't my fault. That's really what I thought! That's the rationalization in the criminal mind. Irreplaceable things had been lost, many students had their education disrupted, a police force spent countless hours searching, a town was taxed for a new building, and I had started the fire, but whose fault was it? Who had forced my thumb to flick that lighter?

I'd moved past Ron Horvath, who eventually left Mount Zion. I focused on my father.

My wife and I haven't been blessed with children, so I can't speak from experience on the difficulties or joys of fatherhood, and the period in which parenting is most physically demanding, those first several years, is the period of life none of us remember. So I can only imagine what my father must have felt when I came rampaging into his life. It would've been difficult for anyone.

But I don't know the formula for raising a son. I don't know the right balance of propriety and intimacy, the firm hand and the gentle. I don't know the right tone of voice, much less the words. I don't know if you're only required to speak when the boy makes a mistake, or if *everything* is a mistake. I don't know if the Bible can stand in for your love, or if the only love that matters is from above, or if you figure the odds are good your son will turn out well, so leave him to his toys and books and imagination. I don't know if you're supposed to be feared, if your son should call you "sir," if there's a limit to the rules by which we should live. I don't know if you should be a mystery, a temple on the mountain, glimpsed with wonder by the children below . . .

I can see, from your faces, this is not the Father's Day sermon you expected, and I apologize, but it's weighing on my heart. And I don't want to list everything my father got wrong, or make excuses for my own mistakes. Everyone has a responsibility to grow up. I had to become my own man.

My method, maybe unbelievably, was to try to find a way to my father. I thought if I could connect with him, make him proud, I would pour cold water on the fire in my past. In college, I called him weekly for brief, breezy chats. When he picked me up for the long drive home at winter break I chiseled at his thick walls—I asked about his past, politics, or the latest loss by the Cleveland Browns. I rarely got more than a sentence in return. Sometimes he just grunted or hummed. I bought a junk motorcycle, thinking we'd work on it, father and son in the garage, hands covered in grease. But he turned this down: He was interested in cars only. When I enrolled in seminary, having found in God the forgiveness I needed, part of me also wanted to impress my father. I hadn't just returned to the flock, I was going to lead it. I was taking what he found most important and making it my own.

Believe me, it's a powerful thing, recognizing that you're lost and want to be found. It takes a self-awareness and humility and honesty that are sorely needed in the world. I stopped smoking and drinking, stopped doing a lot of things I wasn't proud of. I enrolled in a boot camp for the soul.

But I was never comfortable. Something was missing. I felt that even as I cried and cried at the awesome power of the change in my life, even as, by the grace of God, this church chose me to succeed Pastor Virgil when he went home to be with the Lord.

When I gave my first sermon here as the senior pastor, my father was in a back pew. Afterward, he didn't smile or pat my back. There were no tears in his eyes. He just nodded and said, "Not bad."

I never understood him. To this day, I'm hard pressed to *describe* him. I could say he was born a long time ago, in a very different world, to a family that knew hardship and never-ending work. I could say he valued decency and a stiff upper lip above most things. I could say he saw danger in everything. I could say he didn't understand the world, and was cowed by it. Or I could say he was the loneliest person I ever knew. But really, what does any of that mean? Does it help you to measure the man?

The image of him I clung to for years was one I shouldn't have seen. I was in my parents' bedroom when they were away and found under their bed a raggedy box of eight-millimeter films. I was sixteen and curious. I picked one labeled "Honeymoon" and ran to our basement. After figuring out how to start the projector stored there, I turned off the lights and was surprised by the images on the wall. A congregation of old pastel-colored buildings, arranged like a Lego construction over a little bay of blue water. There were choppy shots of a village lane and pink flowers in the sun, all through black dust and grain in the film, and then it cut to a clip of my father standing on a boat moving through the bay. Only I didn't recognize him at first. He wore slim white slacks and a yellow sweater. He had a bushy mustache and brown hair over his ears. He had one foot up on something and the other planted, and stood with a hand on his hip, squinting into the spray from the waves. I hadn't been born yet. His whole life must have seemed to be in front of him. He looked young and carefree, in a part of the world he'd never seen before and would never see again. I always wanted to think of him the way he appeared then: gallant and hopeful, worldly and wise, pleased by all the sun, water, and wind.

And then there I was, many years later, beside his deathbed, and he wanted me to say "cut" on the movie of *his* life.

After all that had happened, all that I'd felt over the years—anger, sadness, and depression, the heavy burden of the secrets I'd kept, all of which found their source, for me, in my father—I could've felt some justice, even satisfaction, from giving him a lethal dose and watching him slip away. Look at history: Haven't lives been taken for less than what I'd suffered? And didn't I want, deep in my soul, to take his life? If God could forgive me of everything terrible and shameful I'd ever done, could He also forgive me for this? Would He believe I was really dispensing mercy? That it was my way of forgiving my father, even as the ghost of my younger self raged in my heart? Could I forgive? Could I be forgiven?

But I didn't give him a lethal dose. I couldn't do what he asked.

I got the bucket and sponge Mama used for bathing him and lifted the comforter to expose his feet. With their dark, spotted skin, boniness, and wispy toes gnarled and scrunched, they resembled goat hooves. Cold shot through me when I touched them, but I held them as I ran the damp sponge over toes, heels, and ankles. Water trickled over his dry skin. And I told him the story I've told you this morning. I wasn't sure that I should or could. It felt selfish and callous, but necessary. My father needed to know that his son could end up in prison, that I'd *already* been in a kind of prison, and that he had been my cause and my jailor. He needed to know the truth, just as we all need to know the truth. As my confession spilled from me I saw his face deflate and tears fill his eyes. He didn't move. He passed three days later, but he looked at me then as though I were the angel of death, and he was ready to go where I led. I kissed his feet, anointed them with my tears, and then said the words I'll say to you now, on this Sunday morning:

Let us pray . . .

# II.

# Email from Dad

---

**M**aria,

Or if you prefer "Lacy," I can use that, but I don't think of you that way, and I don't think I ever will. Hopefully you can understand. I'm not trying to be difficult.

The last time we talked, you said you needed space and you didn't want to hear from me. You have to believe me: I don't want to write this email. I don't know how to write it; I feel embarrassed even trying. But I also didn't have a chance to say what I wanted to say last time, things got so emotional. I know you've told me that no one does email anymore, but unless you can tell me how to fit all this in a text message, we're just going to have to deal with email. It'll spare our thumbs, at least.

This is what I tried to say last time:

I don't think a person's family should determine their life, any more than I think a person's government should—and having been brought to the US as a baby from Soviet Ukraine, I believe this more than most. But I also think that discarding your family is like launching a nuke: It should only be done when there is no other choice. Because family, for better or worse, is all you've got. Believe me, I saw my parents struggle while I was growing up, on their own in a strange country, their family unreachable behind the Iron Curtain. I remember my mother at a loss in a supermarket checkout, when a cashier told her she couldn't use food stamps to buy Kleenex, and I had a bad cold. I remember my father's face turning pimple red as he drove through my school's crowded parking lot, his rusty old Toyota barking like a bronchitic dog, drawing stares. Most days, I took the bus. But they had no one to help them, to guide them through their mystifying new life, to encourage them or commiserate with them. That's what family members are supposed to do, and my experience has been that they're the only ones who will.

But, yes, I know, it's a balancing act—don't turn your back on family, but don't let them rule you, either. Not everyone can pull it off. Including me. I didn't always get along with your grandparents. My father, in particular, insisted that I study economics and be a businessman. Imagine being upset that your child wants to be a computer expert! He didn't see money in it, and he wanted me and my brothers to make money, so that we would never have to worry the way he did, so that we could raise the Rusov name out of the dumps. And even if our name never became great, he at least wanted us to be treated with respect. A lot of parents have that hope for their children.

I'm no different. I know it embarrasses you when I talk about you as a baby, but if you ever have one of your own, you'll know why I keep circling back to that time: There's no feeling like holding your child in your arms for the first time. Plus, newborns have no past; it's only possible to think of their future. And that's exactly what I did. I looked into your scrunched, red, tiny face and saw all the faces you would eventually grow into, and in my mind's eye you were always smiling, having become someone who was loved, happy, secure, and yes, respected. I didn't think, then, that that was an unreasonable dream to have for you. After all, nobody likes to imagine their baby will grow up to live in the gutter of society.

I don't mean that's how I think of you. But you know there are plenty of people who see you that way.

Where I differ from my parents is that I don't have their ingrained dislike of the political left, the residue of suffering under the Soviet system. I'm probably more liberal than you think. Actually, my liberalism is exactly why I'm so torn. I want to support you in whatever choices you make about your life, and I'd always believed they should be your choices and no one else's. I'd always accepted that, as an adult, you are free to manage yourself, unforced by church and state and society, and this alone—this agency—is enough to imbue whatever you do with noble empowerment.

But then I got that email from Robby, your high school guy, with the subject line that hit my gut like a wrecking ball: "Do you know what your daughter is up to?"

Well, no, I didn't. You'd been gone for a year by then.

I'll leave Robby aside—I'd liked him; I thought he was a gentlemanly prom date for you, quiet and doting, but his email was an admittedly ratty thing to do. It hinted at the venom that must exist between you two, about which the less I know, the better. (My hands are full enough with just you.) And it was, in its poisonous way, a quiet, gentlemanly email, just that devastating question for a subject and, in the body, a link to a page at Pornhub.

My body clenched. I began to shiver. If you can believe that. But it's true: I actually shivered, looking at what filled my screen. Because there, in the video's thumbnail—a video entitled "Brazilian Slut Gets Slammed"—was a naked girl who looked like you, staring at the photographer, at tens of thousands of viewers—at *me*—with a look of defiant, inviting pleasure. You wore more makeup than I'd ever seen you wear, and your hair was longer, and the name of the actress tagged in the video was not yours, but it was undeniably, unmistakably you.

Maria. My daughter.

I've never been able to watch porn. Sure, I've seen it. Who hasn't, these days? Anyone with an internet connection has likely been exposed, and I've seen my students giggling over photos on their phones between classes. But I've never been able to get past the discomfort I feel, knowing that the naked women on my screen are daughters, sisters, granddaughters. Or maybe even mothers. And I know that not all of them are there because they really want to be, even if they begged for it and freely signed a contract. Some people look into their future and see nothing, and how am I supposed to forget that? Moral implications are everywhere, and sometimes there's a brokenness at the heart of the enterprise. It's the reason I've never done drugs: I know they're available to us only because someone, somewhere along the supply chain, had to suffer or even die, not as a bug in the program but as a feature, and I see no high in that.

Anyway, the point is, I couldn't look at porn even before I knew you were in it, so you can imagine how impossible it was (and is) for me knowing you're involved.

Still, since I know what people can do with photos and videos, I hoped that what I'd seen was some kind of prank or fluke. It would've been terrible, of course, for someone to do that to you, but it would've been manageable. We could've found a way to deal with it. Maybe someone had stolen photos from your social media to create a fake. So, I typed "Lacy Ayala" into Google and was disheartened by the number of sites it fetched. It was no fluke: I had to close my browser quickly before those images of you—exposed, testing your limits—were burned into my brain.

I've already told you I imagined the faces you would grow into after you were born. But now can you imagine *my* face, after learning what I'd learned about you?

Some days, I miss your mom more than I can say, and that was one of them. I paced around the house, wishing she were there to share the shock, to advise me. I imagine she would've found a way to calm me down. Before her heart disease worsened, when she was the one who needed calming assurances, that was the role she played for me. She played it extremely well. She knew that, like a baby, I just needed to feel her arms around me, and she would offer me the black beauty spot on her collarbone, like an ink blot that had spread and absorbed into her skin. Kissing her there was my comfort. And as for you, she saw you clearly. After all, she'd been a bit of a rebel herself. (Maybe you got it from her? I've never been as comfortable in my skin as you are in yours. Where else could your confidence have come from—pop stars? Somehow, that idea seems disappointing.) Your mom defied her big Catholic Brazilian family to marry a secular Slavic guy—and not even a wealthy one, but a computer teacher at a community college—when she could've had anyone. Maybe she would've tried to convince me that you're a strong woman like her; you just needed to do your own exploring, and you would be fine, in the end.

But then I remind myself: If she were still here, you probably wouldn't be where you are now.

Am I wrong to assume that? Was it strength that brought you to where you are? Was it free will? Would you have traveled the same path if everything had been great at home? These are the questions that keep me up at night now. Plus all the what ifs: What if I'd done this or said that, what if I'd recognized sooner, et cetera. And behind them all is the biggest what if, the one that rings in my head even when I manage to sleep: What if it's my fault?

I know most people's answer to that one. It would be naïve of me to believe that I could have a child in one of the most morally judged professions, in one of the most sanctimonious of societies, and escape judgment, too. So, for the first time in years, I had butterflies in my stomach before I walked into my classroom, because I realized that if Robby knew about you, then probably so did others. Maybe *all* of my students knew, and they'd gorged themselves on videos of you getting who-knows-what done to you. Maybe all of my colleagues knew, too. Maybe I was the subject of their lunchtime whispers among themselves. *You know about his daughter, right?* And then their minds would fill with the worst assumptions. What kind of parent had I been? They could tell you exactly what kind: Instead of giving my daughter puzzles to solve and languages to code and examples to aspire to, I'd given you no guidance, no morals, no happiness, no hope . . .

I used to think I knew your answer to the question of my responsibility, too, but now I'm not so sure. I mean, you did blame me, in so many words, in the note you left when you ran away—*I hate it here, don't bother looking for me.* How did you think I would take that? And you made your feelings about Janice clear before you left, too. But when we talked last time, you were all freedom this and choice that, and it's your life and so on, as if you hadn't felt your home was some kind of sharashka. As if you'd come from no home at all.

About Janice, look: I know what it's like to be young, to feel a burning desire for purity (it's not necessarily a bad desire, it can just lead to messiness), and in your mind, I'd committed some kind of sin. You thought I'd moved on too soon. Or maybe what upset you was that I'd moved on at all. But I'll say this again: I've never stopped loving your mom. You have to believe that. I never can stop loving her. But I have accepted that she's gone. I simply couldn't stay in a gloomy, grieving place. I needed to move on. I would never wish for you to experience the death of a partner, but the sad truth is that you probably won't understand where I'm coming from unless you do. Because there I was, a hardworking widower father of a teenage girl, and along came this eager, thoughtful, loving woman who said, to my complete surprise, she wanted to be part of my life, of *our* lives, and it was like a tugboat had arrived to pull my schooner away from the rocks. So, yes, I welcomed it. I needed it. And I learned: There's more capacity in my heart, and maybe everyone's heart, than I'd thought.

Or that's what I thought I'd learned, anyway. You showed me I might be wrong. With every slammed door, sullen eye roll, silent meal, and random outburst, you showed me that, for some, the heart has its limits, after all.

My mistake was assuming the signals you sent were typical teenage discontent. Another woman had come into our lives, a kind of replacement for your mom, in your eyes, and you wanted me to know, in every possible way, that you disapproved. I got it. I heard you. Really, I did.

I just didn't see how far you would take it.

Despite the message you left, I looked for you. *We* looked—your grandparents, your aunts and uncles and cousins, and Janice did what she could, too. I searched online, but I should've known you would block me from your social media. I checked with your school friends. I called shelters, youth programs. And yes, I spoke to the police, but since you'd left a note, they had no reason to consider you missing. People can go if they want, I was told. I thought you'd probably gone to Manhattan, since I'd taken you there often enough to see the sights. I pictured you begging in Times Square, sleeping in Central Park. It terrified me. I could think of nothing else. Every hour, scenarios invaded my mind, the worst things that could happen to you. Unspeakable things. I'm reminded of those ads I used to see on TV—it's 10 p.m., do you know where your children are? You had just turned eighteen, and I had no idea where you were at any time of the day.

The hole I fell into was deep—insomnia, depression. I kept working, kept smiling at jokes my students made, kept chatting with colleagues about ball games and politics, but, to be honest, I was dead inside. And still I kept digging. Eventually the hole became too deep even for Janice to reach me. I forgot her birthday, what she'd studied in school, the names of friends she'd mentioned a dozen times. Some nights I just turned my back to her and fell asleep. I don't blame her for leaving, which she did sadly, regretfully, sending me her best wishes. Maybe a part of me wanted her to leave, the part of me that fantasizes about moving to a remote place, disconnecting from this ugly world.

Obviously, you'd wanted her to leave, too, but, after I told you, the last time we talked, that she had left me and you blurted "Good," I could hear in your voice that a part of you pitied me. Which means, I think, that maybe, deep down, you blame yourself, which means maybe you aren't where you are now simply as an act of protest. Is that true? Was Janice just a convenient excuse for you to do something you wanted to do anyway? Had you been dreaming about it, biding your time, waiting for the right moment? Because let's be honest: If all you'd wanted was to punish me, there are plenty of ways you could've done it, and most of them don't require you to disrobe for the internet. Maybe you were telling the truth, then: your choice, your life.

When Robby's email landed in my inbox, the shock and dread I felt was mixed with relief—you were still alive; the worst hadn't happened—and curiosity. Not curiosity to see your work (sorry if that disappoints you, though it would disappoint *me* if it did), and not just curiosity about how you'd made it across the country to LA, with no money, as far as I knew, and how you'd lived when you got there. (Did you get help? What story did you tell people? Or did you know someone there, maybe someone you'd met online, a stranger to me?) I mean curiosity about you, this person I'd raised. Someone who, it turned out, had desires and a worldview that I had never ascribed to you, making me wonder if there had been other boys in high school besides Robby. Had I been oblivious? When I taught evening classes, did you bring boys to the house for practice? Did you bring girls, too? When you were out with friends, were you really experimenting in basements, in the backseats of cars? How little I'd known what was happening under my nose! How little I'd known you! You were someone for whom freedom meant something different than what it meant to your grandparents.

Yes, I admit: I thought about your grandparents, as I paced around the house that day and during many of the days that followed. I couldn't let them go on worrying about whether you were alive or safe, and while I wanted to tell them you'd called or emailed, and you were making ends meet working in retail somewhere, part of me felt that if I had to know the truth, then so did they. After all, they'd been lied to their whole lives, and then they came to America and swallowed even more lies. If anyone needed a good, hard dose of truth, it was them. *Here's the free market, you Reaganites; here's what it looks like.* But the first time I saw them after I learned about you, they sat in my car (I drove them to get a new air conditioner), after they'd greeted me in the regretful, melancholy way that had become our norm, and I looked at them with their thick glasses and liver-spotted skin, and I opened my mouth . . . and just couldn't do it. They're of a generation that still feels intense shame about certain things—things that, evidently, a large portion of your generation finds common—and they believe reputation is just as important as money, if not more so. I feared the truth would've devastated them. I still do. I've had plenty of opportunities, but I still haven't told them that I know where you are and how you make your living.

Did you feel the same dread that I would be devastated? When you envisioned my reaction, what did you see? Did you conclude I would be too weak, too lacking in some aspect of character to hear the truth directly from my daughter? Did you merely want to avoid tears (mine, yours), or was it worse than that—was I already dead to you? Had you already consigned me to oblivion and moved on with your life? Is that why the only way I could hear your voice again was to reply to Robby's email and beg him to send me your contact information?

He came through. I don't know how; I didn't ask. And I'm sorry you felt ambushed by my call, but you can understand that I wanted to hear your voice, to hear directly from you that you really were OK, can't you? (Didn't some part of you want to hear from me?)

I know you were frustrated after the call. I was, too. I didn't want to come across like the KGB kicking in your door.

And no, don't worry, I'm not going to show up suddenly in LA. There'll be no rescue mission. I know where you are, and who you are to the world, and that's enough for now.

But I still don't know if you're OK. Actually, I'm pretty sure you're not, no matter how much you might insist otherwise. (Forgive me for sounding like a father, but it's what I am, in the end.) I heard your defenses—that it's art (OK, maybe), that it provides an outlet to people who might otherwise channel their energy into violence (again, maybe), that it's not illegal (true), that, thanks to regular medical testing, it's safe, and it can pay well if you're smart—but I just can't find myself on the same page as you. Plenty of jobs pay well without saddling you with complicated social baggage. And, for most people, I'm not sure that the choice is porn or prison—your audience could channel its energy into art, loving relationships, or any number of things. And marijuana is legal in many places now, but that doesn't mean you should smoke it for a living. You say you've considered the potential consequences, but I'm not sure you have. Because when you tell me some in the industry have found careers in Hollywood, and some have written bestselling books, and plenty of legit celebrities have done nudity, I can't help but think that for every one of those success stories, there have got to be a thousand people who were exploited, pinballed through a cruel machine they didn't fully understand, who ended up bankrupt, homeless, addicted to drugs, imprisoned, or dead well before their time. Or they ended up miserable, social outcasts dealing with the fallout of what seemed like a defensible decision when they were eighteen.

And before you argue that eighteen is old enough to vote and fight in wars and take out loans, I've seen too many older folks lately saying and doing incredibly stupid things to put much store in age. Your grandfather, for one, thinks there are brain-controlling microchips in his flu shot. No matter what decisions we face, few people are old enough, it seems.

Look, basically, I'm not saying you can't, because I can't say you can't. What I'm saying is that if you're going to run a really difficult obstacle course (and, to be clear, even relatively easy lives are obstacle courses; the one you've chosen is almost impossible by comparison, though it might seem like easy money now), then your eyes had better be open.

I think that's what your mom would have told you.

And I know it's not fair: Why can't you just live your life? Why can't you have fun? Why do you have to be on guard? It's society that should change!

Well, I can't speak for society. I'm not sure I'd want to, either. And I don't want to lecture you about morality, but I'll just note that the videos people share online—including the ones that feature you—label the women "sluts" and "whores," and when your audience is constantly calling you a bimbo and much, much worse, it's hard to make the argument for dignified professionalism. That's why it's so hard to succeed once the cameras are done recording you. (And they *will* stop recording you—soon. I did some research: Most people in the industry last only a few years, if they're lucky. Will you make enough money during such a short time span? Like, enough to retire? Because I don't have the money to pay your bills and my own; the payout from your mom's insurance wasn't that much. Or do you think you'll last longer than average? Do you want to?)

I wish our society were different and our lives were easier. I really do. But then, you know, I wish for lots of things I can't have.

Most evenings, after I've finished eating spaghetti or a bowl of Campbell's chicken soup in the glow of the quiet television, the evening news reminding me of all that's wrong in the world, I'll go read in bed, usually a book about the latest revolutionary technology or what the commonplace tech had to overcome to get here. But sometimes I'll pop into your room. And though I've tidied up in there since you left—vacuumed the carpet, dusted the desktop and blinds—sometimes I find one of your long black hairs in a random place, between the pages of one of your books or on the power strip into which your computer and lamps are plugged. And sometimes I can feel you behind me, expectant, impatient as usual. I wish you were there, in your sun-print pink pajamas, asking me if I can figure out what happened to your computer; your game froze just as you were about to beat a difficult level. "You and your games," I'd say. "Are you sure you didn't hit a wrong key by accident?" "I don't hit wrong keys," you'd say, confident, indignant, so beautifully young, reminding me that you know your stuff. Because you're my daughter, because you'd grown up navigating keyboards. And from the kitchen, your mom calls out that dinner is ready: "Come on, slowpokes! Stop playing with your beeps and boops and feast on something real!" And all at once, the smell of roast beef and sweet potatoes comes up from the kitchen, and I say, "We better go down. Don't want to keep Mom waiting." Your shoulders slump. A look of crushing defeat flits over your face, but then you look at me soberly and nod—it's the moment when your game becomes just a game again. The world becomes childish to you, and some part of me is shattered. I want to cup your face between my hands and kiss your forehead and say something I wish I'd said to you every time we were in a room together: "I love you, I love you, I love you . . ."

But I don't stay in your room for very long, indulging in wishes. I go to my bed and read until I fall asleep.

Anyway, your bed is made. The sheets are regularly washed, the pillows plumped. Just like a hotel. You can come stay anytime you want. I promise I won't make it awkward for you.

Dad

# The Death House

My sister was murdered on her twenty-first birthday. She went to a party her friends hosted at the so-called Drama House on her campus—home to the theater program, for which she'd designed some sets—and decided to walk back to her dorm alone, at night, via a riverside path that was not well lit. She never made it home.

A devout Christian, she abstained from dancing and alcohol. She kept mace in her purse. She carried an EpiPen for a mild peanut allergy. Given who she was, I can only assume she went to the party because she liked the people there, and she took that path home because she had walked it at night many times before. I don't imagine she was scared.

Her body was discovered a week later, wrapped in plastic in a crawl space inside an old house about a mile from campus. The police found bones from five other bodies stuffed behind walls or buried in the yard. (Although one skull was found in a rusty bucket in the killer's bedroom, a reporter noted on the local TV news.) The other victims had been dark-skinned prostitutes or junkies, whereas my sister was a blonde, white communications major. For her, media and police attention had been intense.

The media used the killer's full name: Stephen Tarsus Sollanger. I remember thinking it didn't have the evil ring of "Hitler" or "Dahmer." I could see it on a business card or an election ballot, and that's probably the future his parents—upstanding, white middle-class people—had dreamed for him. They had died in a car wreck in the late 1980s, and he'd inherited their house, a narrow, three-story Queen Anne–style home built before the First World War. By the time cops arrived to search for my sister, it was so rotted, so redolent of death, I wonder why it wasn't the first place they looked.

This all happened sixteen years ago. I was twenty-five. I'd just been accepted to NYU Law, and I was riding high. Then a few days later my father called to tell me Becky's friends had reported her missing. I'll never forget my hurried heart as the news sank in, this bunker-buster of reality aimed at my core. I assumed she was dead. I don't know why, for me, the worst outcome surfaced first, but I'm sure other people, in similar situations, have surrendered to the same fear. Still, I felt guilty, like I'd betrayed my sister.

I wish I could say I was close to Becky, that we talked constantly, shared secrets. But after I left for college in Massachusetts, her friend took her to an evangelical conference featuring minor celebrities and Christian rock bands. She was in high school. She converted. Soon after, she emailed that she had dumped her boyfriend because he wanted to sleep with her. I replied that she couldn't expect everyone to share her new faith; if she didn't want sex then she should stick to born-again types. She never responded. Instead, to our parents' bafflement and my own, she became super Christian: summer camps, missionary trips, the whole deal. Suddenly, we spoke different languages. A gulf opened between us.

Her autopsy revealed she was sexually violated after she died. I had to hear this from the medical examiner's report multiple times—in court, in the media—but it only made me vomit the first time, which was a month after the funeral. I was in my Washington Heights apartment, listening to my father on the phone over reggae from a stereo outside. He tried to play it off like good news: She hadn't had to endure it; she was already gone. Apparently that was Sollanger's thing, playing with dead bodies. I put my phone down, tears in my eyes, and knelt before my toilet. I'd teased Becky for her chubbiness as a kid. I thought about her pale skin that bruised with alarming ease—from sitting a certain way for too long, from the most harmless bump against furniture. The thought of some psychopath having his way with her body . . .

I told myself: Get it all out now. Cry, retch, whatever you need. But you *cannot* do this every time, because this story is never going to stop being told.

And sure enough, sixteen years later, I'm back in Ohio, going over it all again.

It's strange to be in my parents' house now that my father is gone. He had a heart attack three years ago. My mom seems too small for this brick Colonial in Mariemont, a rich, quaint old suburb of Cincy, and I have a feeling she's going to sell it. I'm reminded of a Beckett play I saw once in which a man relocates to evade memories of lost love, which of course only makes the pain worse. You can't escape heartache so easily. At the same time, I don't know how my mom manages here. I can't enter what is now a guest room on the second floor without seeing it as Becky kept it—pink canopy bed, Rembrandt prints on the walls, a plain gray hamster cage on the floor. (The room always smelled faintly of hamster pee and wood shavings.) Nor can I sit in the first-floor den without seeing my father on its brown leather couch, reading *Popular Mechanics*, frameless bifocals slipping down his nose, belly surging with each breath. Reading, for him, was a full-body activity: He would rock back and forth, shift to the seat edge, touch his face. When I eat in the sun-filled kitchen I expect him or Becky to burst in, picking up where we left off, a never-ending conversation.

My mom has never spoken publicly about Becky, though the media and various lobbying groups have all asked her to take center stage. She prizes privacy like it confers status—something she's always aspired to have. So when the press camped outside our home, she and my father turned to me. I was going to be a lawyer, they said. I'd know what to say. I figured I was protecting them. I read statements I typed, hands shaking for the cameras. Twenty-five-year-old kid.

My mom's hair is white now. Invited to witness Sollanger's execution, she turned to me. Once again I was asked to represent the family.

Nicole, my wife, was surprisingly in favor of it. Like me, she's against capital punishment. She can spout all the stats on it you want. A program director at Amnesty International, she's published articles on criminal justice.

I told her about Becky on our first date. She asked about my family, but I would've told her regardless. We met for drinks in a hotel bar in Tribeca with a fireplace and well-heeled out-of-towners. It was my first date since Becky had died two years before, and though I was surrounded by law students desperate for stress relief, I hadn't had sex either. I just couldn't. The first night Nicole stayed over I wanted to enjoy our intimacy, but at the sight of her naked body I fell off a cliff, imagining myself debauching a corpse. I was so repulsed, both by the thought and my inability to prevent my brain from having it, that all excitement was lost. That's why I told Nicole: fair warning. She assured me she was full of life and desire, but it took years of frustration and shame before we had our daughter.

In that way, I too am one of Sollanger's victims. A secondhand kind. Nicole has embraced the idea that seeing can heal and watching him die will bring me fully back to life. When I tell her she's being hypocritical, she says sometimes compromise is a sign of maturity, of taking the world as it is, which is, in its own way, a first step toward change.

I'm not so sure. Maybe I'm too vain to admit I'm wrong, but I think my mind can follow a path to healing without being led by my eyes. I know I'm disturbed by what happened to my sister, and I feel guilty about how little I offered her, how I'd wasted the time we had. I know I need to accept these difficult feelings and move on. There will be nothing magical about watching Becky's killer die.

More practically, the execution was scheduled for a Thursday. I'd have to miss work. I'd have to explain my absence to our fourth-grader, Ella. Generally, I don't like lying, but Ella doesn't know yet about her dead aunt.

And yet I said I'd do it, maybe out of morbid curiosity. This is, after all, the most extreme thing my profession does, though I never pursued criminal law—something my friends expected, the victim's brother snaring murderers for a living. No, I work in trusts and estates. Sollanger has given me enough grisly detail for one lifetime, and I've spent too many hours pondering the questions he inspired. Like, did he sneak up on Becky? Did he strangle her there on the path? Or did he pretend to be friendly, in need, and lure her back to his house? Was that the first time he saw her, or had he stalked her? Had he *known* her? These questions haven't been answered. His idiotic defense (he represented himself) was that someone else deposited the bodies when he wasn't home. DNA evidence said otherwise, but he still pleads innocence. Maybe I'm hoping his last words will reveal some truth. Or maybe I want to see if Nicole is right. For all of my high-minded opposition to the death penalty, I was pretty happy when bin Laden was killed, I won't lie. Maybe I'm looking for happiness here, too.

It's an odd feeling, these maybes, this fog in my head.

A lamp gives feeble light from my nightstand. I'm sitting in bed in my old room. The execution is nine hours away.

•

The sun isn't up yet, but my mom sits at her kitchen table, eating grapefruit and browsing the real estate section of the *Enquirer*. She's a retired agent. Plus, the front page has Sollanger coverage. She gives me a loving smile when I walk in. I scan the pantry (what to eat before watching someone die?) and settle on toast and black coffee. My mom is an introvert, and I don't know what to say—I'm not going to unload my anxiety or blurt out how sorry I feel for her—so we eat in silence. She's still at the table when I leave.

It's a two-hour drive to Lucasville, and I haven't driven in more than a year. From the Upper West Side, where Nicole and I live, it's just two stops on the 2/3 train to get to Times Square, near where I work. We don't leave the city often enough to own a car. Out here, though, tell someone you don't have wheels and you're an alien. That's what I feel looking at all the buttons in the black Hyundai I rented at the airport: city versus country. I don't belong here. I never did.

I wonder, passing towering trees on Route 32, if people involved in executions tell themselves they're moving a soul from one plane to another. In New York, I see an occasional subway prophet; here, I see religious bumper stickers and churches left and right. I can understand why Becky converted—hang out in a barbershop, eventually you get a haircut—but if she were here, would she really view death as just a door to more life? If I were pulling the plug on someone, is that what I would tell myself?

I'm convinced Becky lived the only life she got. She isn't looking down from a pink cloud, flapping wings. I wish she were.

And what did I know about her life? Was she in love? Happy? Excited about her future? I don't know.

I'm wrong: Her conversion wasn't inevitable, like a haircut in a barbershop. She was trying to fill the hole I'd left in my wake.

I pushed her onto the path that ended in Sollanger's arms.

I tell myself to ditch these thoughts. I have a role to play. A sign says "Lucasville—Next Exit," and my grip relaxes on the wheel.

I've managed the drive, although traffic is sparse at this hour and Lucasville, it turns out, is a small town.

On the road to the prison I see protestors. They're all ages and races, men and women, silently holding handmade signs behind a littering of candles and flowers on the roadside. EXECUTE JUSTICE, NOT PEOPLE. DON'T KILL IN MY NAME. They're maybe twenty altogether. Diehards. I can't help but admire them. A short distance away are news vans, transmitters lifted like birds stretching their necks.

Across the road, the prison spreads, tan buildings, green acreage. Except for the fences and guard towers, you could mistake it for a community college. It's picturesque, really, in the morning sun. It'll be a beautiful September day, warm and dry. I drive past a brown sign that says SOUTHERN OHIO CORRECTIONAL FACILITY and turn into a full parking lot. The fencing hits me hardest. Barbed wire, imposing. I've never set foot in a prison. My stomach feels like a withered balloon.

Inside, a small reception area has cushioned chairs lining the walls. Two men and a woman, all Black, sit and wait. I approach a desk where a Black woman in a brown guard uniform sits behind Plexiglas, like a cashier at a theater box office. She has a Caesar haircut with orange tips. I tell her my name and show her my ID. She consults a list, then picks up her phone. After a few minutes, a beefy white young man appears. He resembles Jake of Body by Jake fame. He tells me his name but I don't remember it. He welcomes me, says he's with Victim Services, and tells me I'll be taken to a separate waiting room.

Because I'd read the materials the prison sent, I left my phone in the car. The only things I declare to the guards at the metal detector are my wedding ring, belt, wallet, and keys. I pass through soundlessly, and then Jake takes me down a windowless cinder-block hall to a room behind a blue door.

Inside, a Black man sits at a rectangular conference table, hands flat on the wood surface. Like me, he wears a button-down shirt.

He is heavy and on the older side, but I can't guess how old. Bald on top. Mustache. I know he has been staring at his hands, and there is a wary, defeated look in his eyes. I nod and fill a chair across from him. Jake closes the door.

"I'm Gerald," the man says. I decide he is probably an IT guy who has had to introduce himself at countless meetings. I tell him my name.

"I'm here for my cousin," he says.

"My sister," I say.

He nods somberly. I want to ask if he is the only family left or just the only one willing to come, but chatting seems wrong. He goes back to looking at his hands. He doesn't seem happy to be here, but—I don't care if this is selfish—I'm glad he is. I'm not alone; I have an ally.

The door opens. A thin, brown-skinned man walks in, wearing a navy blazer and yellow tie and carrying a clipboard. He wishes us a good morning and says he is Julian from the prison's public relations office. From his accent, I guess that Spanish is his first language. Then Jake walks in. They'll escort us to the death house, Julian says. His black hair is parted on the side, combed, shiny with product. As he talks, he holds his hand out and presses imaginary piano keys. He explains that six reporters will share our viewing room under a strict order of silence. There will be no cameras or phones. On the other side of a wall will be the inmate's witnesses. At no time will we see them. Once the execution is complete, we'll return to sign papers. We'll have the option to make a statement to the press in the prison's media center. When Julian asks if we understand, we nod. When he asks if we have questions, we huddle beneath a blanket of nerves.

To get to the so-called death house, we walk outside. Gerald favors his left leg, so we go slowly. Because our waiting room had no windows, I get a taste of what it must be like to be locked up, to experience daylight as luxurious. Suddenly I feel flush with good fortune—low cholesterol, freedom, dividends accruing in multiple accounts, a wife and daughter missing me. Tonight's weather forecast matters to me. I'll get to experience it.

The death house looks like a two-story storage facility. Flat-roofed, windowless, tan brick. It's surrounded by grass, except for a blacktop drive that leads to its entry: two doors atop a brick platform with stairs on either side. In front of the platform is a big blue scissor lift. For removing the body, I realize.

Sollanger is in there.

I follow Gerald up the stairs. Jake opens a door and we walk into a muggy little hall. Then he guides us through another door into the viewing room. It's dark except for light that spills in from the execution chamber, which I see through a large window. Julian brings us past a black dividing wall. On the left side of the wall are three empty chairs where Sollanger's witnesses will sit. On the right side are three for us. Gerald takes the chair nearest the dividing wall. I take the one next to him. Jake and Julian leave.

Before us is the padded table where Sollanger will die. Restraint straps dangle and armrests poke out. It lies on two metal columns bolted into the floor. "Chamber" seems wrong: The room has a bland, almost corporate feel, with white cinder-block walls and fluorescent lights overhead. A small black clock hangs on the center wall. To the right is a phone and a microphone with a long, stretchy cord. At left, there is a large mirror. It hides the room from which the chemicals will flow. Replace the gurney with desks and I could see telemarketers toiling away in this space. Or a couple of reporters.

The Supreme Court has already declined to hear an appeal. The governor has said he won't intervene. The only drama, I think, will be whether the thing is botched and I end up watching Sollanger writhe. It's happened before. Prisoners scream in anguish. Sometimes it takes forever.

My mouth feels coated with dust. I tell myself I can still leave, but I know I won't.

I want to see this.

I hear footsteps, then chairs scraping floor. Gerald doesn't strike me as prone to outbursts, and I'm certainly not, but it's probably good that there's a wall. I don't want to endure a look from a priest. For the moment, I want to be alone with my thoughts. I hear reporters shuffle in behind us. One sniffles. Another flips through a notepad. I stare straight ahead.

What I do for my clients prepares them for death. It's at the root of all their paperwork, investing, legal protections: this yawning apocalypse toward which they're headed. Me, too. I've tried to look away (I don't even have a will, believe it or not), but it's been staring me in the face my whole life. What will be the last thing I see, a ceiling like this? Fluorescent lights? Is that why I want to witness this, to get a preview of my own end? To be reassured that it could be as easy as falling asleep? Or to be reassured that, just maybe, Becky's end wasn't something I need to feel so terrible about? But I don't feel reassured. It *is* terrible. I imagine what it must be like to know the exact hour ahead of time, and I think I'd be terrified.

When the clock says nine the brown door to the chamber opens. The first person through is an older white man in a black suit, white shirt, and red tie. He resembles Harry Truman: short, good posture, small eyes, thin gray hair. He must be the warden. Behind him is a stout young guard in brown uniform. He grips the bicep of the man behind him—Sollanger. Two guards follow them into the room.

My stomach wrenches. The last time I saw Sollanger was at his sentencing, when, despite his patchy brown beard, he'd struck me as childlike: pale and skinny and with a cowlick. He'd looked at us with bright eyes as if grateful for our interest. Now he is bald, clean-shaven, and heavier. As the guards remove his cuffs and guide him to the table, I don't see any light in his eyes. His face looks scarred and worn, with a hammock of fat under his chin. His name had not conjured evil for me years ago, but now the sight of him does. I wonder if I'm trying to shield myself against what's about to happen—it'll be easier if he's not human.

Stepping onto a stool, Sollanger views his audience. I don't know how well he can see through the glass. Though our eyes don't meet, my forehead burns. Then he turns, sits, and swings his legs onto the table. Two guards ease him back and strap restraints across his arms and body. His head is near me. A man and woman, each white and wearing a suit, enter the chamber. The woman grasps a tube that emerges from an opening beneath the mirror. The man inserts a needle into Sollanger's right forearm and the woman connects the tube. They wear latex gloves. There is no sound while they work.

I stare at Sollanger's face, which I now see in profile. His flat nose, prominent cheekbone. A bluish vein in his temple. He eyes the ceiling, breathing calmly. Does he think about what landed him here? Is he thinking about Becky? Does he, too, believe he's about to see an afterlife? Or does he simply observe an orange water stain in the ceiling and lament the ignominy of it all?

Beside me, Gerald swallows hard. I want to hold his hand. For his sake and mine.

The catheter team leaves with a guard. The warden looks at the remaining guards. One stands by the door and another by the viewing window. Then he lifts the microphone from its wall mount, switches it on, and stands where Sollanger can see him. When he talks, his voice carries thinly through speakers screwed to the wall behind us. I wonder how many times he's had to do this.

"Stephen Tarsus Sollanger," he announces, "the people of the State of Ohio have sentenced you to death. Before your sentence is carried out, do you wish to make a final statement?"

Sollanger licks his lips. The warden positions the microphone.

"Can God create a buckeye so heavy he cannot lift it?" Sollanger says, his voice surprisingly high and youthful. He looks at the warden's perplexed face and adds, "More weight."

When Sollanger gazes at the ceiling again, the disappointed warden switches the microphone off. Gerald looks at his lap and shakes his head. I have to admit: It stings.

The warden nods at the mirror, and I know deadly chemicals have started to flow. I don't know what comes over me. I leap from my chair and bang on the glass. I hear gasps. The warden looks up, alarmed. "That's all?" I shout. "Is that really how you're going out? With defiance? With *quotes*? What right do *you* have to be defiant?" Sollanger, already fading, moves his head in my direction but closes his eyes, like a child who won't respond to his parent's calls to get up for school. "Don't close your eyes!" I say, pounding the window. "Do you hear me? What was the last thing Becky said? Do you hear me?" Someone puts a hand on my shoulder. I hear a different someone saying, "Sir! Sir!" But I can't stop. "What was the last thing she said? I came all this way!" Sollanger's skin turns crimson, his hand shivers. The warden gestures, speaking to a guard. Soon there are hands on both of my shoulders. "Would you even understand if you could hear?" I say. "Did she say she loved me? Just answer that: Did she say she loved me? Nod if you understand!"

A guard pulls a yellow curtain across the window. Our room goes dark. The people who've been trying to pull me away—Jake and a guard—take me by my arms and force me to the back of the room, among the reporters, who stare at me, concerned.

Gerald takes a deep breath and exhales loud and slow. "Good," he whispers.

I don't feel good at all.

When the curtain is pulled back, the warden is beside another old white man in a gray suit, wearing latex gloves and standing over a motionless Sollanger. The warden raises the microphone. "The inmate is deceased," he declares. "Time of death was 9:24 a.m."

I have another few seconds to stare with watery eyes at Sollanger's face. Then Jake says, "Come with me." Angrily, he and the guard lead me out into daylight.

•

I take a detour on the way back to my mom's house. I have time before the flight that will bring me back to Nicole and Ella, whose absence I feel like a stomachache, and I can't deal with my mom just yet. I know the look she will give me, hoping for details, conveying the awfulness of our story. Will the press report my outburst? Will my mom hear about it from TV? Either way, I don't have it in me to narrate like I've just been to one of Ella's school plays. I don't feel like talking at all, actually. Unlike Gerald, I left the prison without facing the press.

There's a tremor in my spine.

What would I have said, standing before reporters?

I thought I might feel sorry for Sollanger. No: I was *hoping* I'd feel sorry for him. That's the feeling hiding like a tiny flame in my fog. I don't need to be told he felt happiness and sadness, tragically lost his parents, wanted to be loved. I know all of that. But on seeing him strapped, diminished, put down like a dog, I wanted sympathy to well up in me. And it didn't. His last words didn't help, but still. It's strange that I can put myself in his shoes and not feel that emotion. I keep searching for it, driving back toward Cincy. I don't know what it says about me that I can't find it. Does that make me normal?

I asked Sollanger the wrong question. It's not whether Becky loved me—I know she did—but whether, despite the distance between us, she knew I loved her, that my cold heart was capable of it. Or maybe that my heart isn't so cold.

For where I'm going I don't need a map. Soon I'm driving down a block of three-story houses left and right, porches with wicker chairs, American flags, faded lawns. A postal carrier in blue uniform lugs a satchel of mail over her shoulder. AC units jut from windows. An older man pulls groceries from the trunk of his sagging Buick. When I get to the end of the block I park by the curb and get out.

Becky's grave is on the other side of town. But this is the place that draws me now, a corner lot of patchy grass and dandelions, a gap in the neighborhood. I think of it as her final place, where my memory of her remains. Usually, I struggle to find Becky's face among my frothy memories, but now I clearly see her round nose, blond bangs, slightly droopy blue eyes—my mom's eyes. Her teeth looked too babyish for her age, tiny spaces between them. I don't want to lose this image of her, though I know I can't make anyone see her the way I do. To Ella, she'll only ever be a story Daddy tells.

The house was razed years ago. I don't know who owns the property. The city? A relative who can't sell and won't build? Nothing indicates that Sollanger lived here, but I'm sure everyone around here knows. Parents must whisper to each other, warn their kids to stay away. Maybe they're worried there are more secrets to unearth. After all these years, it's still redolent of death. I want to post a notice: HE'S BEEN GONE FOR YEARS.

Someone in a noisy red Toyota drives past, eyeing me, a question on his face. I must look like I'm posing for B-roll for a *60 Minutes* segment, leaning against my car, staring at nothing. Or maybe, in the driver's eyes, I'm the dangerous one. Whatever. I guess I'm not normal. The emptiness of the lot—weeds, stray trash—feels good. And the sun, all of its rage, feels so calming, I don't care what anyone thinks. I could stand here forever.

# Frankenstorm

---

During Hurricane Irene, I waited until the meteorologists said the worst was about to hit the city, and then I went out and jogged up the middle of Broadway. I thought it'd be fun. Most people were hunkered down, bathtubs full of water, cupboards full of crackers. (I'm not criticizing—I had thirty-six bottles of water and three boxes of Nilla wafers at home.) I ran from Battery Park, near where I live, up to City Hall and back. Police cars sat curbside flashing lights. I passed a guy walking a brown terrier. No one said, "Hey, lady, don't you know there's a hurricane?" I imagined I was the last defender of New York, staring down a gray Sauron, a destroyer of cities. I felt exhilarated, free . . .

Anyway. It was windy, but then it's always windy here.

I moved to the Financial District in that period after 9/11 when no one wanted to be here. People abandoned million-dollar apartments or sold them for songs. I don't blame them. For a while, passing through on the R line, you could smell dead bodies. I can't even describe it. The air was toxic—I bought one of those surgical masks I always see Asian tourists wearing—but so far I don't have cancer, just a one-bedroom with a view. I've always felt like a 9/11 profiteer. But then I remind myself I've had a tall ladder to climb. It's not like I'm some house-flipping queen who swooped into Ground Zero to make a buck. Living near the disaster was a step up for me.

My grandfather said, "People will tell you that money is evil. Nonsense! Money can make wonderful things happen. You should try to get as much of it as you can." I'd always liked my grandparents better than my parents, who'd taken to driving thousands of miles to visit every Baptist church in America; their zeal was unbearable. My grandfather's zeal, on the other hand, was heartwarming—and surprising, given that he was a KGB officer during the Cold War. I learned this during college. After years of studying reports, he concluded that America was actually pretty nice and escaped to see it for himself. One time I asked him how he had pulled that off, but he shushed me and patted my head.

To be clear: My grandfather was not simply encouraging me to find a rich husband. That was the extent of my mother's ambition for me, but not his. To him, I had two arms, two legs, and a brain; there was no reason why I couldn't make my own money.

My grandfather also said, "Don't be obvious in anything you do." That, too, came from a boyhood under Stalin. I'm sure he could have parlayed his knowledge of Soviet intelligence into a windfall—and maybe he did, for all I know, though he didn't have a lot of cash when he died. He faced a path that led to a big house and flashy cars, maybe a spot on bestseller lists or informing Hollywood movies. Instead he settled in Sea Gate, in a modest house near the ocean, a stone's throw from Little Odessa, where he spent the rest of his working days replacing sparkplugs in the Oldsmobiles of Russian émigrés. Among them could have been bounty hunters and spies—you never knew, and for that reason my grandfather never posed for pictures, and he never made friends.

In those days a mechanic could afford a house in a gated community on Coney Island. Lucky for me—I spent a lot of my summers there. My grandparents kept a bedroom for me. They took me to the amusement park. I loved walking on the boardwalk, sea salt in the wind. Grandma was a water wussy, and only I could convince her to brave the ocean. She deplored my Russian-less tongue, and was always teaching me. "You will thank me someday," she said, and she was right. (Now I'm brought in to work deals with Russian firms.) She was a pretty, roly-poly woman with a booming voice. She read pop philosophy and was jolly in a way I wish I could be. She died from pancreatic cancer in 1998.

I was in New York by then. I'd moved here to study economics at Columbia. My classmates were the children of Wall Street titans or Saudi princes, whereas I had to bag groceries twenty hours a week to help pay tuition. I didn't mind. I knew a slinky sophomore who worked for an escort service; she made more money, but you know. After graduation I became an Excel slave at Lehman Brothers. They expected me to work 24/7, and I thought, who's the whore now? I wasn't too down when the firm imploded, though I met some decent people there. By that point I was at the private equity firm that employs me still.

My grandfather died a month before Hurricane Sandy hit. He had flown to Chicago for Irene the year before—his first time on a plane since he came to America—and was relieved to return to a house that was perfectly fine. (He thought I was crazy for staying; I didn't tell him about my run.) I asked him what he did out there, and he said, "I had a hot dog. Then I went to the top of Sears Tower, and I looked at America." I don't know what I expected—he was eighty years old. Thinking of him shuffling among the crowd on the Magnificent Mile, looking lost, I felt sad. But then I thought, maybe he had a blast. Maybe he saw something inspiring from the top of

Willis Tower. I never found out. Eliciting intimate details or feelings from him was like getting a dog to talk, and I didn't have the touch. Then his heart gave out and it was too late. A mailman spotted him through the living room window, motionless on the floor. I cried so much at the funeral I surprised myself. I'd been proud of my self-control—I barely shed a tear at my grandmother's wake—but there was something about his service, in a little Slavic funeral home in Midwood, with only immediate family and a random sneezer in the audience, that felt profoundly unfair. He'd always seemed so much more of a big deal to me.

My father must have tried closing my grandfather's bank account, because the week after the funeral I received a letter from a lawyer at Bank of America, informing me that the bank had been named executor of my grandfather's estate and his will had been submitted to probate court. I was invited along with my parents to a conference room in the Bank of America Tower, where we listened to the redheaded lawyer read a document none of us had known existed. My grandfather had about nine thousand in savings and a life insurance policy worth fifty grand. He had no investments, no pension. Then came the doozy that scorched my father: The house in Sea Gate was mine.

My heart kind of burped.

At the funeral, my father had said he would call a real estate agent. As next of kin, he assumed the house was his to sell—not a totally unfair assumption. But my parents lived upstate, and my grandfather must have figured I would use the house, since I was based in the city. Or maybe he thought his granddaughter with the fancy economics degree would know what to do. Regardless, I can't deny the happiness that spread through me as the lawyer informed us we had a right to contest the will. I could see the storm in my father's mind—he must have felt he'd done something wrong. I think he was totally destroyed, actually. But, as with all things, he accepted his lot. It wasn't so much his father's will as it was God's, in his view. Plus, suing his own daughter would have been unseemly. After the meeting, he shook my hand like a stranger. I felt bad for him—I almost apologized—but I also felt satisfied.

I found the house on Zillow. What my grandfather must have paid less than one hundred thousand for was now worth about eight hundred thousand. Other homes in the neighborhood had sold for a million. All these blue-collar immigrants, I marveled, sitting on piles of money. I had never viewed the house through that lens; it was always just Grampa's house.

It was about fifteen hundred square feet; two floors; three bedrooms in a shell of off-white siding. It had been built in the mid-1960s and looked like it, from the plush red breakfast bench in the kitchen to the white vinyl floor. My grandparents never remodeled. If the house weren't on Beach 45th Street, an easy stroll to the Atlantic, in what had become a city of middle-class millionaires, I doubt Mr. Market would've blessed it so.

I knew my options: I could sell it as is, or put money into renovation and maybe sell it for a million, or I could rent it out, or I could keep it as my own getaway house. Nothing jumped out as the right choice. I'd always been unsentimental about property—I never understood, for example, why people refused to sell when their homes blocked some development; so what if you had memories there, you can make memories *anywhere*—but I knew my father would be pissed if I sold it, banking a small fortune he felt rightfully belonged to him. (He was too proud to ask if I'd share the proceeds, and I had too much of a conscience to cash out.) On the other hand, I live in an apartment in Manhattan for a reason: A house is a terrifying responsibility.

I spent nights staring at my ceiling and making frequent bathroom trips. At work, I faded in and out of meetings, experiencing sudden intense erotic fantasies. I left my glasses on top of a toilet paper dispenser; I only remembered the Diet Coke I'd left in the office freezer after someone told me the can exploded.

Soon my father started calling. "Did you sign the paperwork the lawyer gave you?" Or, "Have you been by the house yet? Is it still in one piece?" And so on. He'd always been anxious, but now I thought he wanted me to know I was wrong—wrong to have inherited the house, wrong in whatever decision I made. I had *not* been by the house yet, I told him. I hadn't had time. Not that it was his business.

He had never been a big caller, by the way. He was not someone who checked in. It took a big fat inheritance to get him to pick up the phone.

Sometimes I thought I could pinpoint where my relationship with my father turned south—seventh grade, when he, upon discovering a trove of unsent love notes hidden in my Berenstain Bears pencil box, mocked me mercilessly and demanded to meet my secret crush—and sometimes I thought it was silly to boil a relationship down to a single incident. Seventh grade! And he'd done worse since, believe me, including using my credit card without telling me. For a lawnmower. For the record, my father wasn't a drunk or anything, if that matters.

Then one day his phone call was a warning: "There's another hurricane."

OK, I said. So? He could've told me it was a nice day and I would've asked what he wanted me to do about it. Which was unfair, but then so was life, and mine was too full of reports and spreadsheets and meetings and deadlines to worry about the weather. Would I prep the house just in case, my father wanted to know. I don't know, I said, would he recommend the necessary debt portion of the buyout on my plate then, given that Congress had peed in the pool of American credit? He didn't want to hear it, but the thing was, *neither did I.*

Another hurricane, another neon pinwheel on some tanned weatherman's map.

But then the pinwheel came closer, and then it turned toward the city, and then it became "Frankenstorm," and I was like, OK, fine.

I don't normally leave things to the last minute. Actually, I had just taken a personality assessment at work, one of those Myers-Briggs offshoots that tells you what you already know, and I'd gotten high marks for "personal responsibility." But my lowest score? Work-life balance. Which, again, I could've told you. Point is, while everyone was stocking up on water and Oreos, I was neck-deep in due diligence for a meeting with our managing director on what was, it turned out, the day before the storm hit. Which was a Sunday, if you're keeping track. Nobody asked for the day off. In my office, unless you had swine flu or something, you worked; our Sunday was someone else's Monday, after all. At least on Sundays we could wear jeans. Usually.

My father called. "Do I really need to come down there?" he said. "From Poughkeepsie?"

Grumbling, I set out before noon that Monday. The office was miraculously closed because public schools were miraculously closed. An evacuation order had been issued; public transportation was shutting down. People battened down the hatches while I scooted across the Brooklyn Bridge in my silver Jetta, listening to *In Utero* and thinking about how some artists never stop being cool, and why that is. (And also: how I was now exactly the kind of person Kurt Cobain would've despised, and how *that* had happened.) I was shaky behind the wheel, not because I could see the beginnings of the storm around me—granite sky, choppy harbor—but because I rarely drove in the city. In hindsight, I don't know why I felt I needed a car at all—my garage fee alone could've fed a small family every month—but it felt grown up and expedient, I guess, even if I never actually had time for a weekend jaunt to Montauk or the Jersey Shore. I was happy, that Monday, just to make it to Coney Island.

The neighborhood looked deserted, but I knew there were always people who refused to evacuate, no matter how dire the warnings. My grandfather's house (*my* house) oozed abandonment. I hadn't seen it since before the funeral, and now it struck me as dilapidated, eerie. It needed paint, light in the windows. If I'd seen it in a picture I'm not sure I would've recognized it right away. I don't think that's what made it seem eerie, though. Nor was it the fact that my grandfather had died inside it. It was silly to be haunted by such thoughts—everywhere you go, when you come down to it, is a place where someone has died. It was more that I had a sudden feeling that, after opening the front door, I'd know what to do about the house, like it would *tell* me. Sell! Rent! Renovate!

But standing in the entry, all I knew to do was move stuff from the lower floors.

I began in the basement, which was finished in that it had carpeting and a couch. Against one wall was a box metropolis, taped and dusty. With a key, I sliced open one box and found wreaths, gold-laced bulbs wrapped in tissue paper, a plastic angel with a chipped wing. My grandfather hadn't decorated for holidays since my grandmother died. (I think he only ever decorated to indulge her.) I wasn't aware of any stories behind what I saw—like this bulb inspired my great-grandfather in the gulag, or what have you—so I tossed the box aside. In another box I found VHS tapes labeled in my grandfather's wobbly scrawl: Chernobyl documentaries, news broadcasts of the fall of the Soviet Union, presidential inaugurations. My grandfather never owned a video camera, so there were no personal videos. (There were, however, framed pictures of us scattered throughout the first floor, which I planned to collect.) In another box I found dozens of vinyl records, mostly of Russian music. Glinka, Mussorgsky, Tchaikovsky; performances by Chaliapin, Vishnevskaya. I'd known my grandfather admired music, but I hadn't known he was hoarding a collection. That box was a keeper. Another box had a pile of bank statements, receipts, and checking account ledgers, beneath which were two notebooks filled with my grandmother's handwriting. Her Cyrillic taunted me—was it a diary? A memoir? A novel? I could speak Russian but could only barely read it. My father could translate, I figured, and if not, I could hire a student. I held one of the notebooks to my face and breathed it in—it smelled more of damp cotton than my grandmother's Chanel No. 5.

I didn't want to get lost in memories, so after opening a few more boxes and finding only a record player and a shoe-shine kit that were of interest, I lugged my plunder upstairs. It was already dark and raining. Wind whistled past the house. I put on a parka and went outside.

As I opened my passenger door and deposited my grandmother's notebooks on the seat, the storm didn't seem so bad. The wind was bearable; just a skim of water was on the street. I looked forward to sporting flannel PJs and curling up in bed before long.

When I reentered the house, my mother called. Which was typical—my father called about money, my mother about emergencies. Only when I put my phone to my ear all I heard was a garbled murmur as if from a radio with bad wiring. I knew it was Mom saying my name, her voice traveling through a block of frenetic cloud. "I'm here," I said. "Can you hear me?" I got cloud in response. "Mom, we have a bad connection," I said. "I'll call you when I get home." Then, figuring maybe she could hear me just fine, I added, "Everything's OK here. Nothing to worry about." The sound in my ear turned to fizz. I looked at the screen on my phone: still connected. "Hello?" I tried. Then the call ended.

So *that* was unnerving. My parents didn't have cell phones, otherwise I would've texted, but it occurred to me that I should text *someone*, just to announce where I was. You know, just in case. My friend Janice from college, who lived in Rego Park and whom I didn't actually see that much anymore? Robert or Dinesh from work? Lindsay, who was my best friend growing up but who now lived in Oregon? I imagined each getting a message that read, "*I'm @ grampa's house Coney Island. All OK.*" It felt desperate—if I'd gotten such a message, I probably wouldn't have known what to make of it.

I carried the box of records to my car. Across the street, what looked like a swarm of spectral energy gushed from behind the neighbors' houses. I stopped, throat blocked, and watched in disbelief. It was like a CGI effect of evil fog. There was a hiss. Then the flood slammed my shins. The water was freezing, and it didn't stop coming.

(I see this in my dreams now: black ocean washing over everything.)

I dropped the box of records with a splash, ran back to the house. Water rushed through the front door with me. Upstairs, in my grandfather's bedroom, I reached around in the dark until I found the framed photo he had kept by his bed—a sepia-toned wedding portrait, my grandmother wearing a daisy crown, my grandfather in military uniform, neither of them smiling. A totally disappeared world—and not any less so for my saving the photo. But I clutched it like treasure, and as I hurried back downstairs a wind gust rocked the house so hard I felt it shake. Stupid, I told myself as I stepped back into the flood. If I die for a picture . . .

I remembered to close the front door behind me. Rain pummeled me. Suddenly I was wading through the ocean, and the wind sent debris flying. There's no other way to describe it: a long way coming, but all of a sudden.

I ducked into my car, tossed the picture onto my grandmother's notebooks, and slammed the door. Key to ignition. The engine started. I figured the Belt Parkway, which I'd taken on the way in, would be flooded, so instead I'd go up Neptune Avenue to Ocean Parkway, then make a run through high-ground Brooklyn. I started slow, worried about flooding my engine, and outside Sea Gate the water gave way to solid road. Then it was just rain and wind for a couple blocks. Something clanked against my windshield. Kurt Cobain growled from my speakers. My seatbelt alarm kept beeping. I was the only one on the road.

Then I saw a lake ahead—so much for Neptune Avenue. I turned right. I knew Mermaid Avenue would also take me to Ocean

Parkway, but somehow I missed the turn. Traffic lights dangled over the road like bungee jumpers after the plunge. Streetlights flickered. My headlights showed an onrush of rain. I futzed with my car's GPS, but it couldn't even locate me, let alone tell me where to go. After what must have been only a minute I found myself kicking up water again, and the blackness in front of me was the ocean. I'd driven all the way to Surf Avenue, by the beach. There the water poured in like a dam had been busted. It covered my headlights. Panic, I discovered in that moment, is like a lightning strike that shorts your mind. I may as well have driven off the edge of the earth.

I looked left up the avenue, hoping to see pavement (it, too, could've taken me to Ocean Parkway), but all I saw was rain and water and darkness. Having no choice, I put my car in reverse and hit the gas, but I heard a gurgling cough from the engine, a struggle like bolts coming loose, and then, to my horror, my smart little hatchback died. I hurt my fingers twisting my key, pumping the gas and hoping for a spark, but it was no use. The water outside was level with my hood. It sloshed and slapped with the wind.

"OK," I said, trying to calm myself, "OK . . ."

It sounded like I'd parked under a waterfall. My lower half was soaked and freezing. I wasn't sure if it was better to remove my shoes and socks or leave them on, so I left them on. Surrounding me were big empty spaces—parking lots, I guessed—with tall apartment buildings another block or so in each direction. I saw lights in one building and took full breaths like a deep-sea diver preparing to submerge. I thought I'd open my door and make my way toward the lit building, press all the intercom buttons until someone let me in. But then there was a loud crack and a spiderweb appeared in my passenger window, and I remembered the YouTube videos I'd seen of the Japanese tsunami the year before, people swept up in the monstrous flood like tree branches, and my door stayed shut.

My phone had a weak signal, so I dialed 911, knowing full well that it was idiots like me who were pulling first responders away from fires and heart attacks during what was surely a worst-case-scenario night for emergency services. I got a busy signal. I listened to it for a minute and then hung up.

The water outside my door looked *hungry*. Maybe it had reached its high point, I thought. Maybe if I just sit here . . .

But what if I needed to pee? Was it better to hold it for as long as I could, spend the night in a piss-soaked car, or risk the elements?

What if all the water receded as quickly as it came in? When, exactly, was the tide? I lived on an island but had no idea how water worked.

I roused my phone again, opened my Facebook app, and posted a status update: *If anyone is near Coney Island Beach and willing to help, I'm stuck and in serious trouble.* I am not one of those people with thousands of Facebook friends, but of the ones I have, many live in the city. A tiny hatchling of hope tried to break through its shell. I stared at the screen, refreshing the page, until James Mauricio, whom I barely knew in high school and who had become the beer-bellied manager of a Sunglass Hut in a mall outside Albany, commented, "Call 911." When another jerk liked my status, I closed the app and tried 911 again.

Busy signal.

I fumed. If I couldn't get through because some clown was complaining about his satellite reception . . .

I closed my eyes, took more deep breaths.

I was going to be OK, I decided. Also, if the need arose, I would just pee on the floor—which, I realized, was already wet. I thought it was from my drenched feet, and then I leaned over and touched my palm to the floor on the passenger side, totally submerging my hand. Two inches of water, at least. It was coming in.

"This is not a problem," I said out loud. "Everything's going to be OK."

I moved my grandparents' stuff to the backseat, and then, with a seat recline and rusty limbs (I'd always hated those perfect little bony girls with their yoga mats, but now I wished I was one), I ended up there, too. Knowing exactly what I would find, I checked the floor again. Then I sat against a door with my legs on the seat and my stuff on my belly and argued with myself. What exactly prevented me from just opening a door and swim-walking to safety? Was there really such a good chance of being swept up in a current or impaled by flying glass? Well, I reminded myself, there *was* such a chance, in fact. Maybe not good, but a chance. And opening a door would completely ruin my car, whereas otherwise I had a shot at making it through with manageable water damage. Also, I wouldn't be able to keep my grandmother's notebooks dry outside, not until the rain stopped. But these reasons weren't good enough. I could afford a new car, and I hadn't known my grandmother's notebooks existed until that afternoon. What if they contained grammar exercises or baking recipes? I mean, seriously. What was I talking about?

I checked my phone: no service.

Through all the noise I heard a steady clanging—a flagpole pulley rattling inside its metal truck. It reminded me of the most terrifying music I'd ever heard, in an artsy film I saw in a theater once: Buddhist monks in a Tibetan monastery in India, guttural chanting, depressed notes, horns like charging ships in triumphant disaster, and a dull bell clanging. It had sounded like death, and I was hearing it again, there in the middle of the storm. In high school, enraged and lonely, I'd put a handful of sleeping pills in my mouth, but couldn't bring myself to swallow. In case you want to know. I played that scenario out more times than I care to admit, eulogizing myself, rationalizing. In another few billion years the sun will die, and everything we've ever done will have been for nothing—so what difference did it make if I drowned in a Volkswagen on Coney Island? There were worse ways to go, and I'd had a pretty good life. I'd never been raped or assaulted, never been shackled to a sewing machine to make rich people's underwear, never foraged landfills to survive, never been awakened by bombs falling on my village.

I'd had enough comfort to be bothered by the little things, like not being asked to senior prom, like never having birthday parties, like having never been to California.

But I wasn't going to die, I told myself. I didn't even *want* to die anymore, and don't think that wasn't a hard fight. Don't think it wasn't *still* a fight.

The bell kept clanging; the wind bellowed.

The water was level with my seat; I could smell it now, pungent with salt and gasoline. I needed air: It felt like it was seeping from the car and it was harder to breathe; I just needed to *breathe.* Forgetfully, I pressed the button to lower the window behind me. It was shut tight. On my knees, I searched the window opposite and found a tiny opening. I rummaged in my purse for my ritzy titanium credit card (don't judge), which I used to shimmy the pane enough to fit my fingers. But pushing a car window down, I discovered, was much harder than I would've guessed. I bruised my palms. I screamed. And when it was finally down, I was spent.

The water didn't wait, though. I had to get out.

Cursing my stupidity, I wrapped my hood tight, pocketed my phone, placed my purse and grandparents' things on the roof of the car, and then exited through the window like a NASCAR champion. It wasn't easy. Rain in my face, water lapping my butt, and my arms tired, I needed adrenaline and I don't know what else. I was sure I'd fall in the water and drown, and a list of regrets zipped through my head—I'd spent too much time worrying about my thighs; too much of my life not liking myself; I hadn't traveled enough; I hadn't cared about changing the world; I hadn't had nearly enough sex; I had made terrible decisions with the few boyfriends I'd had; I was too much a product of my surroundings; I'd never told anyone how badly I was hurting; things could've been very different; I could've been happier, and there was no good reason why I wasn't. These thoughts were embarrassing, and I regretted that, too—who had taught me it was embarrassing to be serious?

I thought: When water hit my lungs, would it hurt? Would it taste awful? Would I fight it? For how long?

But then I got up on the roof on my stomach like a performing seal, tucked the picture and notebooks into my parka and curled up, back to the wind. No one was around. Streetlights were dark. Behind me, in the distance, was a sunset glow, though the sun had been down for hours. It took me a minute to realize it was a fire.

My phone said I had service, so I dialed 911 again. A woman answered. I screamed at her: "I'm stuck on top of my car! The water's coming up!"

Calmly, the woman asked my location, and when I told her, she said all units were busy, but I should stay where I was and help would soon be on the way. Something inside me caved like a soggy ceiling, and when I asked the dispatcher to please hurry, it was with a sob in my throat. She had other calls, so I put my phone away. With the need suddenly desperate, I peed myself. I barely felt it. Then I curled up and lay still. If the water keeps rising, I thought, I'll just jump in.

My body tensed, expecting a glass shard to lodge in my back. For a while, I imagined a rusty nail in my spine, envisioning what I would do, until it seemed useless and morbid to worry about it. I took up such a small amount of space in the world. The odds . . .

I was so wet, and the wind was so strong, I felt naked. Frozen. From somewhere shouting rose up. Teenagers or twenty-some-things. They hollered and laughed, invincible, and I remembered it was almost Halloween. I was seven the last time I'd worn a Halloween costume—I was Snow White. I hadn't felt well the whole evening, knocking on people's doors, but I ate some of the candy they gave me anyway, and by the time I got home I was shivering. My mother rubbed Vicks on my sternum (Vicks was her cure for everything), and my father tucked me into bed. I could see his face: his high forehead, pudgy nose, and brown eyes calm like he was tying shoelaces or chewing cud. Boredom was his normal face.

His hair was just beginning to sprout gray. Seeing me shake, he had put a blanket on top of my comforter, then sat on the bed and sang under his breath. I don't remember the song, just the sound, high and soft. The Vicks pierced my nose with mint. I experienced an intense feeling of love, of wanting to bury my face in him. Instead, I sat up and vomited on his shirt. He picked me up under my arms and carried me to a bathroom, where he washed my face and threw his clothes into a hamper. Then he brought me back to bed, changed the blanket, and tucked me in again. "Feel better?" he asked. I nodded. It felt good to be in bed and I was slipping fast. My father probably figured I couldn't hear him or that I wouldn't remember, but he said, "Good girl. I hope you grow up to be a pretty woman with big boobs, because that's all you'll need in life. Otherwise, no one will ever let you throw up on them. I don't make the rules, I'm just telling you . . ." His voice seemed far away, or I was moving somehow. His face had become dark. Everything was dark. I didn't know where I was going.

When I woke up, I saw daylight, a queasy gray glow. Wind clanged the flagpole pulley and sent ripples through the muddy green water that still surrounded me. It had receded some. I sat up and unzipped my parka, removed my purse, the portrait of my grandparents, and my grandmother's notebooks, damp but not much worse for the wear. The streets were still empty. So much for rescue. My hands shook. They looked puffy and wrinkled like coral. How on earth I had managed to fall asleep, I don't know. I stretched to see into my car, which was smeared with a layer of what looked like feces. Water everywhere. A total loss. It would be the same back at the house. But there would be time to deal with insurance companies and paperwork. I didn't care about who owed whom. I didn't even care about what was in my grandmother's notebooks (my grandfather's memories of Russia, it turned out), or how I'd get to dry land. For the moment I just surveyed the blasted landscape—overturned vans, dead traffic lights, the exposed bellies of little motorboats. Now I was on an island in a calm sea. It was a beautiful morning.

# Sworn Statement

---

IN THE STATE OF NEW YORK
IN THE COUNTY OF KINGS

**I,** Michael Murenko, residing at 833 Slepak Street, Brooklyn, NY, 11223, do hereby affirm the following to be true:

I am eighteen years of age. I have resided at my current address with my mother, Olena Kovalenko, for twelve years.

Katerina Vorontsova, now deceased, formerly residing at 832 Slepak Street, was an acquaintance of my mother and myself. She resided across the street, in a single-family house.

I first became aware of Katerina on or about February 20, 2014, when she knocked on the front door of our house. Later, my mother informed me that, up until that time, she had also not been aware of Katerina—we had not seen her move in, nor had we seen her in front of her house or elsewhere in the neighborhood. On that day, her knocking occurred sometime after 10 p.m., because I was asleep in my upstairs bedroom. It was loud and rapid, and it awakened me. After quickly dressing, I went downstairs in time to see my mother, in a bathrobe, open the door. I heard Katerina say in accented English, "Help me! Please, let me hide here! Just for an hour!"

My mother is an immigrant from Ukraine. She is divorced from my father, who owns a jewelry store in Manhattan. The divorce occurred when I was five years old, so I have few memories of their relationship. Yet my mother seemed to sympathize with Katerina, or relate to her obvious panic, and she allowed her into our house without question. After seeing no one else outside, my mother closed and locked our door.

Katerina was a middle-aged woman of average build, with brown, gray-streaked hair in a ponytail. She sat on our living room couch, wringing her hands and rocking back and forth. She was teary-eyed and upset, but neither her clothes nor her hair was disheveled, and I saw no sign that she was physically injured.

My mother asked what was wrong, and Katerina responded to the effect that her husband had "gone crazy" and was very angry with her. My mother then asked if Katerina's husband knew that she was in our house, and Katerina responded that she had escaped without her husband's knowledge. My mother then asked, "Do you want me to call the police?" Katerina insisted that she did not want the police involved, that her husband merely had a temper and he would cool down after an hour or so. At that point, my mother asked me to return to bed.

From my bedroom, with my door open, I heard some of their conversation. My mother offered Katerina water, which she accepted. She then asked Katerina's name, which Katerina provided. On learning my mother's name, Katerina asked about her origins. Hearing the response, she said, "I knew it. I am Russian. We are like sisters." To which my mother only hummed.

The rest of the conversation that I was able to hear was unremarkable. My mother asked which house Katerina lived in, and was surprised to hear that she lived across the street. Katerina said that she had lived there for almost a year, and that she worked in a supermarket, though I did not hear which one. If they spoke in more detail about Katerina's husband, I did not hear it. However, I did remain awake until she left, fearing that her husband would discover her whereabouts and attempt to enter our house.

The next morning, before I left for school and my mother left for work (she is a stylist at Joseph's Hair Salon in Brooklyn), I asked her about the conversation she had had with Katerina. My mother has always been what I would describe as chatty, both with me and her customers. I have observed her at work, and she talks continuously while she cuts hair. Her favorite topics of conversation are local—she likes to discuss changes to our neighborhood or city, as well as the latest news about people she knows, such as whether someone is getting married, doing home renovations, or has experienced an illness or death in the family. She also loves to gossip about celebrities. I mention this to demonstrate that, in response to my question about Katerina that morning, she was unusually quiet. She told me only what I had already overheard—Katerina's name, ethnicity, residence, and job. When I asked about Katerina's husband, my mother said she did not ask Katerina about him. When I asked if Katerina might be in danger, my mother merely shrugged and said, "Sometimes the people you love are hard to be around."

I assumed she was referring to something she would have been embarrassed to discuss, either 1) her own marriage to my father, who I judge to be a difficult person, or 2) the relationships of our neighbors. There are a lot of Slavic people in our part of Brooklyn. Many of them either fled the Soviet Union or are the children or grandchildren of Soviet immigrants, and unfortunately, I have heard numerous stories from friends about alcohol abuse, domestic violence, and other issues in their homes. I viewed Katerina as the victim of such a scenario. I guessed her husband had had too much to drink and frightened her.

In the days that followed, I looked closely at Katerina's house on my way to and from school. Also, when I was home, I occasionally looked at it through my bedroom window, but at no time during that period did I see her or anyone else on the property.

The next time I saw Katerina was approximately one week later, on or about February 28, 2014. Once again, she knocked frantically on our front door. It was sometime between 7:30 and 8 p.m., because my mother and I were watching *Jeopardy!* on our living room TV. My mother opened the door, and Katerina stood there, wearing only slippers, sweatpants, and a sweatshirt, though it was snowing. Blood ran from her nose, and she was crying. My mother urged her to come inside and then ordered me to get a towel. When I returned to the living room with a clean washcloth, Katerina was sitting on our couch, still crying. As I handed her the towel, she looked at me, and I could see that she was red and sore under her left eye. I assumed she had been assaulted.

My mother sat beside Katerina, comforting her. She gave me additional tasks—to fetch an ice pack, then a cup of tea—I think to be able to speak privately with Katerina. I was not able to hear what they discussed when I was not in the room. When I was present, and after Katerina had calmed down and her nose had stopped bleeding, my mother asked again if she should call the police, and when Katerina once again insisted that she did not want police involvement, my mother said that Katerina ought to, that it was "ridiculous" not to, that the situation was clearly dangerous. But Katerina was adamant that police involvement was unnecessary, that her husband was a "lovely" man who had a temper, and he had simply gotten some bad news connected to his work. My mother asked about his job, and Katerina said that he was a day trader, buying and selling stocks from their home. She added that he, too, was Russian.

"OK," my mother said, "so he had bad day at work. What's it got to do with you?"

Katerina, with the ice pack pressed to her left eye, responded: "Please. No police."

I thought Katerina had avoided the question because she was hiding something. I agreed with my mother: The right thing to do was to call the police.

After a couple of hours of TV and awkward small talk, when Katerina finally said her husband had probably gone to bed and she went back home, my mother and I watched from our window as she entered her house. We saw no sign of her husband. I told my mother the situation was terrible, and she agreed. She apologized that I had to witness such an ugly thing. I asked why we had to keep letting her into our home, and suggested that maybe Katerina would be forced to call the police if we kept our door closed to her. My mother frowned and shook her head. She is not religious, but she said, "You're supposed to love your neighbors. Or at least be nice, you know." After a moment, she added, "Plus, what if her husband finds her when she's knocking here? I don't want someone killed on our doorstep." She then told me that, when she was a girl, she had seen a man stab his girlfriend in the gut during an argument in the street, and she had never forgotten it.

I understood my mother's fears, and for the next week I said nothing about the matter.

Then, on or about March 6, 2014, I was walking back to our house from the nearest subway station, coming home from school in the afternoon. It was cold and raining hard, and I used an umbrella. As I neared my house, Katerina emerged from the front door of her house and shouted, "Hey!" She wore only a casual dress that struck me as inappropriate for the weather, and she had no umbrella. Nevertheless, she hurried out to meet me in the street, repeatedly shouting for my attention, though I had already stopped and was looking at her. In her hand was a white towel. I assumed she had once again been frightened out of her house, but when she reached me, I saw no sign that she was injured or in distress. The bruise beneath her eye was now barely noticeable. She was merely soaking wet. She handed me the towel and said, "For your mama. Please give to her." I looked at the towel, which was also soaked. At first, I could not understand why she would give my mother a wet towel, but then I understood that she meant to replace the one she had used for her bloody nose the week before. I said something to the effect that I understood and would give the towel to my mother, and I thanked her. She thanked me, and then she looked at me for a moment, smiling, rain spattering her face. She grabbed my arm and, while caressing my bicep, said, "Oy, you are strong man already! Such a strong young man!" My eighteenth birthday was still nearly a month away. I had become used to adults, particularly family members, commenting on my appearance, or how much I had grown, and so on. But in this case, since Katerina had not seen me grow up, I thought she was insinuating that I should share my umbrella with her, that it would be the manly thing to do. Yet, before I could offer her my umbrella, she said, "You want to come in for coffee? You drink coffee yet?" I did drink coffee, and a hot drink would have been welcome, but I did not want to go into her house. I did not know if her husband was there, and even if he were not home, I did not want to take the chance of being there when he returned. At the same time, I did not want to hurt Katerina's feelings, because I pitied her and recognized that she may have been in sore need of company. Seeing that I was at a loss, Katerina laughed and said, "I'm just kidding! You don't worry! Maybe next time!" She waved at me, then turned and hurried back to her house. I entered my house, thinking the encounter had been odd and my mother, who was still at work, would find it funny when I told her, which she did.

Approximately a week passed. My mother did not mention Katerina. In general, while my mother is chatty, she is not necessarily friendly, in that she has rarely invited anyone to our house, nor does she visit with people outside of her family, either in their homes or elsewhere. Plus, given what was reported in the news around that time about the Russian invasion of Crimea, I had even less expectation that my mother would make any effort to acknowledge Katerina, much less seek her out. My mother has not been to Ukraine since she was an adolescent, but she still feels a strong attachment to it. She frequently prepares Ukrainian food, for instance.

I continued, occasionally, to look at Katerina's house from my bedroom window. One night, on or about March 15, 2014, as I was preparing to go to sleep, I saw Katerina in a window on the second floor of her house. There were no curtains or blinds on the window, and it was lit. At first, Katerina appeared to be tidying up, moving into view of the window and then out, concentrating on something in the room. I would have stopped watching and gone to sleep, but I was curious if her husband would appear, so I turned off the light in my room and kept watching. Soon, Katerina began unbuttoning her shirt. I assumed that she, too, was getting ready for bed, and if so, then her husband would likely appear, so I remained at my window. But within seconds Katerina had removed both her shirt and her bra and stood naked from the waist up, stretching her arms over her head. She made no attempt to hide from the window, and her room remained lit. I had no desire to see her undressed, but I was so surprised I could not move. She began to sway in a kind of dancing motion, making me think that she was listening to music. This continued for several minutes, with Katerina moving all over the room, until finally she stopped in front of the window and put her hands on her hips. Fearing that I would be detected, I moved away from my window and lay in bed. I did not look out my window again for the rest of that night.

What I had seen was inexplicable to me. I questioned whether Katerina was aware that I was observing her. I thought it extremely unlikely, but not impossible. And, if she had seen me, I wondered about her motivation for exposing herself. I also considered that Katerina may just have been a strange person who enjoyed dancing topless. Maybe, for example, she had been a stripper in the past. Or, possibly, she performed that evening for her husband, who had remained out of my sight. Whatever the explanation, I felt I had seen something I was not supposed to see, and I was too embarrassed and afraid to tell my mother. I thought she would confront Katerina, and I did not want to be the cause of more drama in either of their lives. Nor did I want drama. I was approaching my birthday and high school graduation, and I wanted to celebrate both without the awkwardness that would come from my mother knowing what I had seen.

As it turned out, I did not see Katerina again until April 3, 2014, one day after my birthday. That night, my mother and I were watching a movie in our living room when there was a fast, loud knocking on our front door. My mother looked at me, exhaled heavily, and said, "Here we go again."

After opening the door, my mother gasped in horror. Then she turned to me and yelled, "Quickly! Get towel!"

I bolted from my seat, grabbed a hand towel from our kitchen. At the front door, I saw Katerina on our landing, holding her left wrist with her right hand, blood dripping from her hands. She was crying. When I handed the towel to my mother, she told Katerina to reveal her injury, and that was when I saw that Katerina had suffered a severe wound to her left wrist. An open gash, diagonal across the inside of the wrist, was bleeding profusely. I was disturbed and terrified. I thought there was a chance Katerina might not survive without immediate medical attention. My mother wrapped the towel around the injury. She asked how it had occurred, and Katerina, looking at me, said it was her fault, she had been careless with a knife.

My mother, now pressing the towel to the wound, seeing that it was quickly soaked through with blood, turned to me and said, "Call 911."

I began to turn.

"No!" Katerina shouted. I stopped. "Please," she said, "no police!"

My mother shouted angrily, "I cannot fix this! *You* cannot fix this! You need ambulance!"

Katerina looked down at her injury. "I cannot pay for ambulance," she said.

My mother seemed taken aback.

"Well, you need a doctor," she said.

She thought for a moment, then ordered me to get a plastic bag. I found one in our kitchen, and my mother placed it over Katerina's left hand so it would catch her dripping blood. Then, putting on her shoes, she said she would drive Katerina to Coney Island Hospital. My mother's car was parked in its usual place in front of our house. With Katerina still crying and holding the bag and towel over her wound, they left.

I remained in the doorway, trying to calm down. I looked at Katerina's house in the evening dark. I thought I might see her husband in one of the lit windows, because with all the shouting my mother and Katerina had done, he would have known where to look and would, I assumed, be curious to know what had happened to his wife. But I saw no one. I pictured Katerina's husband, after having slashed her with a knife, sitting at a dining table to finish a meal, or lounging on a couch to watch TV. I pictured him having dismissed her completely, forcing her to become a problem for strangers, and I became incensed thinking anyone could be so cruel toward someone they had promised to love.

I put my shoes on. I want to state, for the record, that I have never been involved in altercations or disciplinary situations. My school record shows no suspensions, detentions, or demerits. I had never been arrested or even so much as questioned by a police officer. In fact, I would say I have been fairly well liked by everyone with whom I have had contact, because I detest confrontations and take care to avoid them. So, as I marched across the street to Katerina's house, I recognized that I was behaving out of character. I told myself I would merely inform Katerina's husband, in case he was interested to know, that my mother had driven his wife to a hospital, taking care not to name which one, so he could not go after her. But I knew, deep down, I had other motivations. I wanted to see this monstrous man, to look into the eyes of someone capable of such animal behavior, if for no other reason than to know to avoid him if I ever saw him. And I wanted him to know, even though we had not called the police, that his actions were known, and he was upsetting more people than just his wife. In the end, I wanted him to feel afraid and ashamed.

I did not think he would feel threatened. I am a thin teenager who rarely works out and plays no sports. As mentioned, I have never been confrontational, so I had no real experience with it. I worried my anger would sound laughable. Stepping onto Katerina's property, I shivered with fear. I reminded myself that her husband, at the very least, had a knife. But, for all I knew, he had other weapons in his possession as well, or he may have been a significantly larger man than me. Then, as I mounted the front steps, light from the windows showed drops of Katerina's blood there, and I nearly turned around. But my outrage guided my fist to knock on the door.

I waited, noting there were no signs of dogs or security cameras.

I remember debating what to say when Mr. Vorontsova answered the door, whether I should sound as angry as I felt or opt for a more neighborly, friendly tone, as if what had happened to Katerina had been merely an accident. It occurred to me that I knew nothing about Katerina's husband. He might have been a violent criminal, even a mobster or a sociopath. I recalled a movie, *The Silence of the Lambs*, in which the main character unknowingly knocks on the door of a serial killer. But it was not a helpful thing to think about. I breathed deeply, told myself I was getting carried away.

After a minute, I knocked again, louder this time.

When there was no response, I considered that Katerina's husband could be out of hearing range—in a shower upstairs, for instance. Or it was possible that he had left the house through a back door. I tried to see into the house through a window, hoping to find evidence that Katerina's husband was there, but because of the angle from the steps, I was not able to see much. Relieved, I went home.

That was the only time I ever set foot on Katerina's property.

When my mother returned, after having watched Katerina, her wound now stitched and dressed, reenter her house, I asked her what had happened at the hospital. She informed me that Katerina had told the emergency staff she had suffered the injury while slicing food. My mother believed the staff were skeptical, but she did not contradict or question Katerina in front of them, figuring it was not her place to do so.

I did not tell my mother about knocking on Katerina's door. I assumed she would be upset with me for taking such a risk.

Instead, at dinner the next day I asked my mother if we should defy Katerina's wishes and call the police. My mother had been quiet and morose all day; I knew she was disturbed by what had happened the day before. I was, too. I had had the unpleasant task of washing Katerina's blood off our front steps. Possibly, I had asked a question my mother had been debating in her mind. She did not say this to me, but I suspected that if she had not been an immigrant, if she had grown up an American and had been raised with an emphasis on free speech, the right to protest, et cetera, or if she had not felt a need to be perceived as uninvolved in such sad affairs, she might not have been so hesitant. So, I told my mother that it was possible to call anonymously, and it was not necessary to provide details that could betray our identity. We could simply ask the police to conduct a welfare check. But my mother responded that people were not idiots; if the police showed up at their door, they would know who had turned them in.

We sat mutely for a minute.

I said, "Why would that be so bad?"

My thinking was that we had not been friends with Katerina; she had only appeared in our lives when she experienced an emergency. So, we would lose nothing if she became upset with us or broke off contact. If anything, she would gain some amount of protection against her husband.

My mother responded, "Because she will stop thinking of us as a safe place. She will have no safe place. And maybe neither will we."

She said it with finality.

I assumed my mother was approaching the situation from a woman's perspective. Or maybe she was recalling the stabbing she said she had witnessed as a child. Whatever her motivation, I did not understand or agree with her position—I dreaded spending every day worried about what emergency Katerina would bring into our lives—but I nodded in response and finished my dinner.

For the next two weeks, I did not see Katerina as I left or returned to our house, or when I looked at her house from my bedroom window.

Then, on the night of April 18, 2014, I saw a police car parked in front of Katerina's house. I was looking through my bedroom window, and I thought I could also see that the front door of Katerina's house was open, but I could not be sure. As I looked, another police car arrived, this one with its emergency lights flashing.

I ran downstairs and told my mother. She went to our front window and looked out.

"Did you call them?" she asked me.

I told her no. I said maybe Katerina herself had finally called.

We continued to watch as an ambulance arrived, and then another police car. Our home and the whole block filled with red and blue flashing lights.

When my mother saw that other neighbors had emerged from their homes, she told me to stay in the house and then she went outside. I stood in our doorway and watched her talk to a police officer. At one point, she put her hand over her mouth. When she returned, she looked stunned and dismayed.

I asked her what had happened.

Sitting on our couch, she told me that Katerina was deceased, that she had missed work or a meeting, or in any case someone had called in their concern, and a police officer had found her body in her home. She had been stabbed in the heart. My mother said she asked if the husband had been apprehended, and the officer told her they had no record that Katerina lived with anyone; hers was the only name associated with 832 Slepak Street.

I, too, was stunned.

I asked how it could be, but my mother remained silent, looking numb.

Together, we watched from our window as Katerina's body, enclosed in a black coroner's bag, was removed from her house.

In subsequent media coverage, we learned that Katerina had never been married, nor did she work in a supermarket. She was the daughter of an executive at an oil and gas company in Russia. The authorities were treating her death as a suicide.

Given what had been reported, I was surprised to receive a visit at my home from Detective Reznik of the New York Police Department on April 19, 2014, at approximately 3 p.m. During the interview, for which legal counsel was not present, he asked if I had ever been in Katerina's house or had had any meetings with her without my mother's knowledge. I stated that I had not. He then showed me several pieces of paper, each encased in a plastic sleeve, that he said had been recovered from Katerina's bedroom. Two contained attempts at drawing a male face in both pencil and pen. The face resembled mine. One sheet simply had my first name handwritten in blue pen. I told the detective that I had never seen those pieces of paper before, nor could I explain why Katerina had them. The detective said that it appeared Katerina may have been infatuated with me. I explained that my interactions with her had been limited to situations where she had approached either my mother or me, usually by knocking on our door. I had believed she was married, because that was what she had told us. It had never occurred to me that I might be the object of her interest.

I have not received any further inquiries from the police, but I want to submit this statement to make the record of my interactions with Katerina absolutely clear. I view her as an obviously and tragically troubled person, and I have been disturbed by her death, and the subsequent revelations about her life and behavior, since learning about them. I have had trouble sleeping and concentrating. Everyone I know has asked me about this matter, and I have found it depressing to discuss. Yet, I maintain that if I bear any responsibility for Katerina's fate—and on this, my mother shares my feeling—it is only in my failure to insist that Katerina seek professional help, or to arrange for that help to be provided to her, though she was clearly in need of it.

SIGNED: Michael Murenko          DATE: April 23, 2014

IN WITNESS WHEREOF, I have hereunto set my hand and seal this 23rd day of April, 2014.

Andriy Babiak
NOTARY PUBLIC

# Świnica

---

According to legend, the spirit of the Polish king Bolesław the Brave rests in a mountain massif near the country's southern border, waiting until he's needed to defend his people once again. The massif is called Giewont, and from a certain angle it really does look like the profile of someone at rest: Three peaks represent chin, nose, and brow. From the tallest, the nose, you can supposedly see all of Poland. Atop this rocky schnoz, nine hundred years after Bolesław's reign, highlanders erected a giant iron cross, claiming the mountain—and Poland—for Christianity. Today, Giewont is a pilgrimage site, a Polish Mount Rushmore. Its peaks are perpetually crowded with proud Poles and selfie-taking tourists.

But the mountain I'm attempting is taller, more difficult, and four miles east: Świnica. The name comes from the Polish word for pig.

It's not that I have no interest in stepping on a royal face, and, I'll admit, I'm prone to tourist traps and harbor a deep-seated desire to do the popular thing. It's just that Świnica is the mountain I have to climb, because, fifteen years ago, my first attempt failed.

Back then, two guys came with me: Ken the Canadian and Klaus the German. We were in a summer language program in Kraków and decided to explore the Tatras one Saturday in late July. I was used to Midwestern plains; it was the first time I saw real mountains, and I was awed. Ancient, majestic rock, sunlight rolling down craggy green faces. In the cable car we took to the top of Kasprowy Wierch, my friends asked if my backpack contained a sweater or hiking shoes. I wore a T-shirt and shorts; all I carried was a ham sandwich and a copy of Nadine Gordimer's *The Conservationist*. It was the first hint, to them and to me, of my woeful provinciality. I mean, who goes mountain climbing in a T-shirt and Keds? But the weather on Kasprowy was fine, warm with a breeze. I thought I'd be OK.

As we climbed, the surrounding beauty made me giddy: To the south, in the distance, the mountains looked blue. An old man in a yellow lambswool sweater and knee-high socks passed us going down, tapping rocks with a wooden walking stick. We stopped for lunch on a grassy slope overlooking a pristine little lake. By the time we pushed on, a steady wind had picked up. Ken noticed my hands in my pockets and offered me a spare windbreaker from his pack. Embarrassed, grateful, I put it on.

The sky grayed, my ears froze. I had been caught in blizzards and thunderstorms at home, but there was no doorway to duck into here, no awning for cover. With little except boulders all around, I was exposed. Wind flattened the camel-hair grass that grows at that altitude. I sheathed one hand in a sleeve and protected my ear. But the roaring wind kept gripping my chest, squeezing my lungs. Looking south, I saw dark, roiling clouds pulsing with lightning, swallowing the mountaintops in their path. Ken and Klaus stopped and stared. "We have to go down!" Ken shouted. Klaus scanned for shelter, but all he had to do was look at me. We were maybe fifteen minutes from the top, but I watched that storm coming at me, and the thought of being inside it, where lightning exploded and wind whipped back and forth, got me moving the other way. When we returned to the path to Kasprowy, breathless and frightened, Świnica was all black clouds. Like a victorious yawp, thunder cracked the air with violence I felt in my feet.

I used this experience for a short story in which a nanny hikes the Tatras to keep an eye on the boy she was paid to watch, and when the storm appears, the boy insists on staying on the mountain. They huddle under a rock outcropping, watching leaden clouds envelop them until all is wind, lightning, and rain, and the boy cops a feel when the nanny holds him in her arms. Years later, the nanny thinks she sees the boy, now a man, as she's selling roses by the Vistula River in Kraków, but by then her mind is addled and who knows what she sees. That story got me into a prestigious MFA program, but all I see in it now is the penchant I had for writing about things I didn't understand.

I don't know what became of Ken the Canadian. But several years later, after I'd moved to New York City, Klaus emailed. We exchanged brief updates. As far as I know, he's still a lawyer in Dresden. Maybe he's haunted by these mountains, like I am. But more likely he's seen bigger or more beautiful ones or he just doesn't care. More likely I'm the only one of us stuck in the past.

The weather on Kasprowy now is just as fine as it had been fifteen years ago, but I know how quickly it can change. It's October. I'm wearing layers and a cap. My beard is thick, hands gloved. People are sparse on the trail from the cable car station. Further east, I see the snow-capped High Tatras, dark velvety ripples of earth. Passing clouds cause kaleidoscopic displays of shadow and light on surrounding peaks. I hope to spot deer or a mountain goat.

But the lack of fellow climbers makes Giewont loom larger in my mind. Fear of missing out, I guess. This is only my second time in Poland, and who knows if I'll come back. In another fifteen years, I'll be too old to climb mountains.

Of course, the second I have that thought I remember from fifteen years ago the old man with walking stick and Trachten socks. He was older than I'll be in fifteen years. Is he still alive? Still climbing?

I don't know why I came here the first time. My father escaped the country, under mysterious circumstances, before Solidarity happened. To ensure I would feel like a real American (though I was born in Ohio), he taught me no Polish. English has always been my only language, and I regret it. So, in part, I'd hoped that seeing my father's country would help me understand him, and in part I'd wanted to learn the language he'd kept from me. But I don't know if you can understand the past by touring the present, or if a birthplace can really illuminate someone's character. I guess, in part, I'd just wanted a new experience.

The day before I left, my father appeared in my bedroom. He worked second shift as a welder, and I had a summer job at the local bookstore, so we were rarely home at the same time. He came in smelling of paint fumes, sweat stains on his shirt, sandy hair mussed. He was shorter than me and less substantial, physically, than the impression I had of him.

"You're going to have a visitor in Poland." He had this smile like I was going to meet Santa. "My son," he said. "Your half-brother."

Everything froze.

"I have a half-brother?"

I was annoyed, thinking he really thought this revelation a treat, but now I see in his delighted eyes the look of a man dangling from a ledge. How else to tell your son about your failed first marriage when what God hath brought together no man can tear asunder? How else to utter old secrets in the new world?

Yes, I had a half-brother: Filip. He lived in Warsaw, where my father had been born. He worked at an airport, and he was married with two kids. Like my father, he was an evangelical Christian. He spoke no English. He would visit for my last day in the country.

Suddenly my father's middle-of-the-night Polish murmurs from the kitchen made sense—phone calls home. I'd always thought he was praying or reading his Bible aloud. I asked for the full story, but he demurred, saying he would tell me someday, a promise that, like many of his promises, remains unfulfilled.

Because my father had left for America when Filip was a toddler, Filip had no memory of him, and neither man had enough money to arrange a meeting. Thirty-five years had passed. And then, with only a cursory debrief, my father tasked me with delivering gifts for his grandkids. He'd already bought the gifts. Filip already planned to meet me.

At passport control in Kraków's airport, I fantasized that scanning me in sent Filip an alert. In my language classes, I heard him in my ear, asking questions I couldn't answer. In the Stare Miasto I kept checking over my shoulder. On Świnica, I felt him shaking his head at me: *You should've been better prepared.* He was around every corner, in the air.

I'd wanted a break from my family. My parents attended a megachurch, Grace Cathedral, housed at a vast television studio once known as the Cathedral of Tomorrow. The pastor was Ernest Angley, a televangelist with plastic-looking hair who made a living assuring Africans that AIDS could be healed. After every service, we ate at Cathedral Buffet, the church's banquet center, still in seventies décor. The food was cheap because the staff was unpaid—long after I moved to New York, a federal judge shut the place down. My father, for one, had loved eating there. I had not, and when I left for college I left the church, too, convinced it was all bunk. My parents and I constantly tussled over it. They thought I was really ditching them, not the faith. In any case, I'd gotten tired of arguing. Poland was four thousand miles away.

But family walked into my hostel in Kraków and asked for me at the front desk. I couldn't wriggle out of it.

My fear, as I descended three flights of stairs, was that there'd be an embarrassing display before all the passersby: touchy, teary, and loud. Filip had known about me all along, my father had revealed. He had heard about my progress in school, my guitar playing, summer jobs, scholarship offers, but I had only just found out he existed. I hadn't even seen a photo. Still, I reminded myself that we were about to play out a moment from Filip's dreams. I wore jeans and a buttoned shirt tucked in. I'd showered and shaved.

In the lobby, at the foot of the stairs, I stopped. He stood at the reception desk across the way, wearing charcoal slacks, a brown suitcase in one hand. He was tall with a paunch; he had a brown beard and thin hair. At the sight of me, he nodded and approached like a drill sergeant inspecting his recruit.

"Would you like to go to the mountains?" he whispered in Polish.

I looked at his round face, chubby red cheeks, brown eyes set in puffy boxer's sockets. As far as family resemblance, I wouldn't have picked him out of a crowd. What, actually, was he asking? It was the day after our failure at Świnica. Had he heard my itinerary from my father? From the desk attendant? Was this small talk?

"I was in the mountains yesterday," I said.

He shook his head, eyes shut, disappointed.

"Would you like to go to the mountains?" he repeated, slower.

I stammered in Polish: "I was in the mountains yesterday."

"Nie," he said, and scanned the lobby, looking, I thought, for help. "Come," he said, gesturing to follow him.

We took an elevator from the communist era; it rattled as it inched along. I expected Filip to examine me, but when I glanced at him, his eyes were forward and down. I thought, *It's going to be twenty-four hours of this.* We'd just met and already I'd screwed up. Why hadn't my father told me more? Why had he saddled me with this burden when all I'd wanted was summer adventure? What would Filip and I talk about? What *could* we talk about? Would he preach if I said I liked Polish beer? He was an airport baggage handler who ran summer Bible camps; I brought a Gordimer novel to the mountains. I imagined committing a verbal stabbing: *My father didn't tell me about you until he had to—you weren't worth mentioning.* I ground my teeth. *Our* father. This is my brother, I reminded myself. This is my brother; this is my brother . . .

After keying into my door, I watched him assess my tiny room—a twin-size bed in the corner, my luggage against a wall, a small writing desk, a window with a view of trees. The room was all white sheetrock and wood. Bed made, towels folded. He put his suitcase on the desk. I closed the door.

"I have gifts for your children," I said, a sentence I had practiced, and made for my suitcase, where I had the toy cars and teddy bears my father had bought. But Filip blocked me, waved the idea away like I'd committed a faux pas.

Then he gathered me in for a hug so long and forceful I might as well have been his long-lost dad.

I know: Plenty of writers would describe that hug better, and the thing is, I've wanted to write about it for years—his grip, his breath in my ear, the smell of his clothes, the thoughts and emotions running through me. But the truth is I don't remember any of that. I can't put myself in that room again.

And anyway, I'm done with writing.

My memory isn't all bad, though: A vista opens and a spark ignites in the part of my brain that holds the pristine little lake where I had lunch fifteen years ago. Here it is: still little, still pristine. It will look exactly like this long after I'm gone. It's a good spot for water and a protein bar, so I drop my backpack, sit in the grass. Wind ripples the lake, wavering a turquoise-and-emerald shimmer at its edges, a play of liquid and light. Miles away, the village of Zakopane is a blur on a lush green plain.

*Would you like to go to the mountains?*

Of course, he didn't point or rephrase, just assumed I'd discern the difference between "to the mountains" (na góry) and "upstairs" (na górę). He was like our father: forgetting to put himself in my shoes. At a surprisingly swanky McDonald's on Floriańska Street, he mumbled through his fingers about his mother. With a mouthful of fries. I'd grown tired of asking him to repeat himself. I never got the story.

I should've said yes: I *would* like to go to the mountains. Up here it's just you, rocks, and weather, even when climbers surround you. Leaving my lakeside rest, I look for others on the trail, but find no one. My thighs announce their tiredness. They'll feel worse in the morning, I'm sure. A cold gust snaps at my face.

Nobody knows I'm here, including my father. My whole life I've told people where I am, where I'm going—I'll just be over here, I'm going to the bathroom, I'm currently out of the office, I'll be back in a minute. This constant registration, this by-your-leave. Is it childish to be so careful? Or reckless to return to Poland without telling anyone?

Filip is in his fifties now. I don't know if I'd recognize him. I certainly wouldn't understand him: I haven't spoken a word of Polish in over a decade.

Would he recognize me? Fleshier, worn, wearing bitterness and failure like a coat. (I could've been a doctor! A lawyer! I could've spent my nights out, meeting women! What did I sacrifice for—a trash bin full of pages?) Jobless now by choice, tired of taking crap from customers. Alone. Would he sniff sadness on me, see buzzards circling? Would he deny our blood connection? In him, I fear I'd see a little boy ravaged by fatherlessness, the Iron Curtain's collateral damage. *Look*, he'd say, *I'm trying to find a hand to hold! I've been trying so hard for years!*

Like I said, my father has never explained why he left Poland without his son. He isn't a sharer, nor is he my friend—he would think the notion peculiar. To him, fathers are authority figures, not companions. That was another way Filip was like him: inspecting, judging, ready to enforce a rule even before it's been broken.

In the years after my first Poland trip, my mother, who is also Polish, referred to Filip with contempt, if she mentioned him at all. Examples of her kindness abound, but for this chapter in my father's story she has no pleasant words. I thought she was jealous—he had loved another woman, maybe still pined for her. Years passed before I realized that my mother simply doesn't know what happened, either. She is with me in the dark, flailing for a pull chain to light a bulb.

Like father, like son: Now I'm the one keeping secrets.

I see comforting circles—half white, half red—painted on boulders, marking the path to the top of Świnica. Some steps stretch my hamstrings, and I regret not buying a walking stick in the village. Also, the path hugs a sheer face—looking down to my right I see how far I'd fall, dashing against rock. A strong wind sweeps through. I stop to absorb it and notice something I don't remember from fifteen years ago: a chain running through rings hammered into the mountainside. Grateful, I grab it and scan the clouds as I round a ridge. At the chain's end the path widens. In another two weeks everything here will be under snow.

It would be so good to be back at my hotel, a bowl of beef stew steaming my face.

But I can't stop. I just can't.

I understand sunk costs. Pushing ahead with a bum manuscript, a professor once told me, is not going to justify—or recover—the time you put into it. He was trying to tell me I don't have what it takes, but I didn't listen. I thought I knew what people wanted—mix drama with humor, embrace strangeness (but not *too* much), end with profound ambiguity—and I didn't want to fit a mold. I wasn't a bum; I was swimming upstream.

Maybe it's genetic, my stubborn arrogance, because Filip had it, too. The morning after he arrived, we toured the Wieliczka Salt Mine, a massive underground complex that had provided Europe with salt for eight hundred years. It contains four full-sized chapels the miners carved, including chandeliers made entirely of salt crystal and a spot-on replica of Leonardo's *The Last Supper*. There are chiseled statues of kings and popes, murals depicting legends, stalactites falling like tears into blue saline lakes. It was incredible, but what stands out most in my mind is Filip scolding a boy who had run into him while we walked a dim passageway: "Don't you know how to walk?" It was some kid having careless fun. When the boy's father butted in, Filip said, "Are you watching your child or not?" His lecture echoed throughout the mine.

I've had better tours. Plus, the tour guide spoke no English.

Above ground, Filip's mood brightened. We went to central Kraków, where we circled the Sukiennice, a grand hall of yellow brick, ghoulish faces lining its roof. In the square, people sold fruit and tchotchkes beneath huge cloth umbrellas. Pigeons flapped their wings and startled tourists. I remember asking Filip what kind of music he liked, anticipating hymns or a favorite gospel group, but he said he liked jazz. I told him I was surprised. He had mentioned that Levi's jeans were the rage among Poles, clamoring for anything American. It occurred to me that he viewed me through that lens—maybe, in his eyes, I was cool.

But more likely he saw me as lost, and "jazz" was the answer he thought I'd want to hear. My leaving the church must've bothered my father enough that he told Filip. So I'm certain my half-brother had gingerly skirted a wound, but I wasn't wise then to the ways even the most devout believers tiptoe around belief with people like me.

Also, I wouldn't have been able to explain myself in Polish.

I'm limping now. My right leg suddenly feels as though the cartilage has slipped from between each joint, leaving bones to grind. I stop walking, rub my thigh. To prepare for this trek, I'd walked a daily lap around Prospect Park for a month, upping to two laps—seven miles—the week before I left. I'd felt fine. But handling this pain is going to take all the Zen I have in me. I don't have ibuprofen. And there's still the journey down.

The summit is within sight. Tufts of brown grass line the path, but otherwise everything is slate-gray rock. Climbers have left their faded marks: *JM – 23.7.98*; *Vasily was here*; *Xiaoming – 13.8.06*; *Jesus Saves*; *Alex G. was here*; *Frank + Anna 4ever*. In small, steady lines, there's a rejoicing stick figure next to English words: *Conquered the pig!* I don't have anything to write with, but even if I did, I don't feel the need. No one would know who I am, anyway.

Still, I allow myself a triumphant look back toward holy Giewont to see if I can spot a human ant line winding up to its white cross. "Defend his people again" my butt; where was the once-and-future king when Germany invaded? But I can't tell which one is Giewont. There is just the green tossed sheet the mountains make of the land.

What I see is someone coming: a man rounding the ridge onto the path where the chain rail ends. I squint against the sun and wind. He is white, tall and with some heft, and appears to have a white beard. He wears a khaki baseball cap, leans on a black walking stick. It's late in the season; I hadn't expected much company. How long has he been following me? He is maybe five minutes behind at a good pace.

He waves.

I gasp—does he recognize me? I raise my hand foolishly, squint harder. He walks with confidence and agility, as if the path is familiar.

It's not possible; it can't be Filip. The coincidence would be gargantuan. I stare a moment longer with mouth open, catching wind. He wears a blue weatherproof parka. I can't fully see his face.

I turn and move, wincing with each step. (When did my body get away from me?) It seems I'll only have a few minutes to myself at the top and I want to enjoy my solitude.

But it can't be Filip. I'd said goodbye to him. After we returned to the hostel from the central square, I went to a graduation ceremony for my language program. He stood with arms crossed at the back of a bright cafeteria and nodded when I received a certificate from the program director. He looked bemused, knowing how poorly I spoke his language, and left as I posed for pictures with Ken the Canadian, Klaus the German, classmates, and teachers. We had crackers and wine, exchanged email addresses. Most of us would never see each other again. When I returned to the lobby, he was at the front desk, settling his bill. "You are leaving?" I asked. When he nodded, I asked him to wait, then ran upstairs, relieved and melancholic. I came back cradling the toy cars and teddy bears for his kids. He stuffed them into his suitcase. Bashfully, he pulled a disposable camera from his pants pocket and gave it to the desk attendant. We posed for the only picture he took during his visit: his arm around my shoulders but no smile. Then we walked to a bus stop a block away. I said I would tell our father everything about him; he said he would tell his children about me. As if I were an explorer who'd landed on an alien planet, made contact, and was now heading back. Considering the costs involved, Filip would never meet his father in person, I knew. (It's odd, given this, that he'd asked no questions about him. I would've answered!) I was as close as he would ever get. Maybe that's why, as the bus approached that would take him back to his life, and he said, "Do widzenia," goodbye, I said what I'd heard our father say many times: "Z Bogiem." Go with God. A message from our father through my apostate mouth.

Filip beamed and hugged me, and I was awash in shame.

It colors everything, that feeling of pitiful surrender, as I hobble onto the summit. Surrounding peaks seem like menacing shards, cold and angry; thin white clouds are the exhaust we give off, collecting overhead, the frigid wind an insistent reminder that I don't belong up here, with nothing but rock and sunlight. I don't belong in this land.

My follower is out of sight now, but he's coming. A few more steps. Nothing I can do about it.

Then everything goes white, like a thick milk sheet has dropped over my eyes. I hold my hands out, feeling. "I'd said goodbye," I say, determined to speak my thoughts despite my sudden blindness. "I don't know why I said what I said. I wasn't revealing anything or talking down, I wasn't accommodating, it just came out. It was goodbye. I was leaving you behind—*goodbye*. And no, I'm sorry, I didn't want to see you again. I don't know you; I don't even know how to reach you. I came back for the mountain, and this was supposed to be mine. Can I just have this little reset? This go back and do it again? Or should I have climbed Giewont after all? Would that have been better? Would you have followed me there, too?"

There is silence, and I realize I'm not even actually on the mountain. Wouldn't I be able to see it? I'm not in Poland—I can't see that, either. I'm in New York, sitting in my overheated shoebox apartment, in front of a blank page on my glowing computer screen, overlooking a quiet avenue. It's the middle of the night. Or maybe I'm in both places at once? Some clouded zone between life and fiction? Embarrassed at myself, my stupid questions, my feeble, idiotic words, trying to turn myself into something to be passed down?

But, fine, whatever, forget it. This needs to end.

Let's say the old climber mounts the last step, and my sight returns as quickly as it had gone: I see his face full of confusion and concern. Thick hair covers his jaw and neck. His eyes are blue. He's no one I recognize. Breath fills his whole body, whereas I can't seem to get enough air. "Co jest nie tak?" he says, approaching with a cautious, friendly hand outstretched, his stick dropped with a clatter. "Co jest nie tak?"

Here, where I am, he never stops asking the question. And what if, though his words seem unintelligible—no one has spoken Polish to me in decades—somehow, perfectly, I always understand?

# Acknowledgments

_____

Three of the stories in this book were previously published, and I'm grateful to the teams at *The Carolina Quarterly*, *Evergreen Review*, and *The Saint Ann's Review*, which featured those works.

I had no expectation that the staff behind the Iron Horse Prize would embrace this book, so my unending gratitude goes to Katie Cortese, Travis Snyder, Leslie Jill Patterson, and all their colleagues at *Iron Horse Literary Review* and Texas Tech University Press for honoring this collection and expertly shepherding it into the world.

Finally, my family, as well as my teachers, friends, and colleagues from Rochester, Syracuse, Columbia, and Barnard, have encouraged me in numerous ways, and I'm thankful for their understanding and support over the years.

# About the Author

---

**Paul Linczak** was born in Ohio. He was educated at the University of Rochester, the Jagiellonian University, and Syracuse University, where he was a Cornelia Carhart Ward Fellow in the MFA program. His short fiction has appeared in *The Carolina Quarterly*, *Evergreen Review*, *Fiction International*, *Meridian*, and other publications. He lives in New York City.